JOEY & OTHER STORIES

BANDANA SHARMA

For Radhika

Contents

Acknowledgements

This book owes its existence to my parents Krishna Priya and Maheshwar Dayal Sharma and my brother, Ravindra Kumar Sharma who shaped my imagination and provided me liberal education. I am especially grateful to my husband, Lakshmi Raj Sharma, whose encouragement and help made this book possible. Thanks to my son, Dhruv Raj Sharma, for his valuable time and suggestions.

Bandana Sharma.

January 9, 2025.

1

Mrs. Hussain

Things seemed to be going well for Akshay Chatterji; his mother had not overreacted to his Punjabi bride, Winnie; Winnie had even brought him luck, for when they returned from their honeymoon he was offered a good job in a reputed carpet company in Mirzapur.

There were some problems, initially. Mirzapur being a small town, accommodation was hard to come by. Akshay had seen a number of flats but didn't find them suitable. Then, as if by providence, the chief engineer of the electricity department was transferred and Akshay and Winnie moved into his charming bungalow overlooking the Ganga in the posh Civil Lines area. To their left was the elitist Mirzapur Club, well-appointed with a billiards table, a bar, a library and a swimming-pool. Winnie, a fitness fiend, was thrilled about the pool. To their right stood the spacious bungalow of the Hussains, only a hibiscus hedge dividing them. Mrs. Hussain was a widow who lived with her daughters and sons.

Akshay's anxieties about Winnie's boredom in a small town were allayed by the hectic rounds of parties on their arrival. Mirzapur was small but it had carpet industries and the highly paid executives who ran the factories met regularly at parties to ward off small town blues. The Chatterjees had fitted in well into the cocktail circuit. Life seemed to smile on them. And then, Akshay's father died. His mother, who hadn't shed a tear, tried to commit suicide by jumping off the terrace. She was saved in time. When she tried to do it a second time Akshay was at his wits end. His mother refused to move out of Chandernagar where she had spent thirty two years with her husband. She could not be left alone in her present condition. Akshay kept extending his leave, hoping she would agree to accompany him to Mirzapur. But she would have none of it. Her husband's sudden death had made her bitter about everything, including her only offspring who had married against her wishes.

The only way out for Akshay was to give his mother a dose of her own medicine. He threatened suicide if she didn't stop making life hell for him. At first Mrs. Chatterjee took this as an empty threat and said, "Do whatever you like, I will not leave Chandernagar." But then she saw how miserable he was. So when he said, "It is not as if I am not shattered by Baba's death, and you are adding to my problems," she agreed to accompany him. But she made it very clear that she was leaving home only temporarily. This was also a precautionary statement – she wasn't too sure about Winnie.

Back in Mirzapur, Akshay's problems were not exactly over. His mother's behaviour had begun to embarrass him; not suicidal any more, she had taken refuge in sullenness. She would not reply his questions easily, nor eat food when offered. Winnie, whose predilections lay more in aerobics than in managing high strung women, soon stopped cajoling her to eat.

Akshay was, frankly, not prepared for this kind of a situation. His father had been one of the best doctors of Chandernagar. It had been smooth sailing for the family. His mother, in fact, was known for her love for life. For Durga, her husband had been more of a friend than a husband. He enjoyed her cheerful banter, even her tantrums. And there was enough money to satisfy her love for expensive saris and plants. After his clinic hours they would play cards late into the night.

This fretful widow in white was not the turn of events Akshay had been prepared for. His heart broke to see her like this. But he was also annoyed with her. Why could she not have widowed gracefully like so many women he knew? And what was the need for her to behave like an ancient Hindu widow! Akshay was worried about what his friends and colleagues would make of her. They would never know from the way she dressed and looked that his father was a Fellow of the Royal College of Physicians, London, and she the daughter of one of the richest and best families of Bengal. She could pass off as any ordinary woman in those dull saris of hers.

Akshay was also worried about what Winnie would think of his mother; her own mother, Mrs. Chopra was the president of Delhi's Women Golfers' Association and also ran a successful boutique in South Delhi. She was more glamorous than Winnie herself. Akshay decided to talk to his mother:

"I am your only son, Ma. This is your home now...so you must try to adjust to it."

Durga looked at him defiantly but said not a word.

"We cannot get Baba back but it will give me immense happiness to see you less unhappy. If you start going out, meeting people, you will feel better."

"And meet whom," asked Durga somewhat angrily.

"Why, there are so many good people here. You could begin with the Hussains. They always enquire after you."

(It was a fact that Mrs. Hussain Sr., had expressed a desire to meet Mrs. Chatterjee, but Akshay, not being sure of his mother's behaviour, had discouraged her with "Actually my mother is too upset to meet anybody.")

Durga, who had decided to be difficult, anyway, now got a reason to be cross. She glared at

Akshay, saying,

"I, a Vaisnava, am going to meet those beef-eating Muslims who broke our idols! Had I known you lived next doors to a Muslim, I would never have crossed your footstep!"

Akshay was taken aback. He had never known his mother to have such prejudices, certainly not when his father was alive – which was just twenty days ago. He had not known narrow-mindedness or hatred to be a part of her nature at all. Had it lain buried in her, to surface when father was gone? Durga was determined to never meet the Muslims next door.

Not before long, one morning, when Akshay had left for office and Winnie for the market, the house-help ushered in Mrs. Hussain. Durga quickly collected herself. She found herself stumbling into the drawing-room and greeting with folded hands a graceful lady in a white cotton sari.

Fatima Hussain was fiftyish, not tall but tallish, not plump but plumpish, on the darker side but not dark. Her wavy hair that refused to stay in place could have given her a casual, easy-going air; but there was an air of patience about her which made her look very dignified.

Durga's defenses fell before Mrs. Hussain's gentleness and composure. She took her pallu to her eyes and wept.

When she recovered, Durga found Mrs. Hussain wiping a quiet tear as she said:

"Your loss cannot be compensated for. But life has to be lived, somehow. Please do divert your mind a little."

The two women talked as if they had long known each other. As Mrs. Hussain got up to leave, she said:

"I will look forward to your coming to our place tomorrow. If you don't come I shall come and fetch you."

Durga felt that such an invitation could not be resisted.

The Hussains welcomed her with such warmth that Durga felt regretful that she had stayed away from them all this time.

The Hussains' was a relaxed household. You could visit them any time and not find anyone in a hurry to do anything. Fatima Hussain was of course a widow. There were in the house, two unhandsome good-natured sons with warm smiling faces. The elder one was married to a sweet young thing who made excellent tea. (Durga could not help comparing her to Winnie who looked athletic and determined every morning, in her slacks and sports shoes.) There were also two talkative young daughters waiting for marriage.

The Hussain women did not go out much. They struck gold in Durga who was a wizard at knitting and embroidery. The boys had complained good humouredly about the datedness of their sweater designs. Durga modernised the girls' knitting projects. Such designs Mirzapur had never seen. Before long a whole new world of household skills opened up: recipes were exchanged and joint ventures were planned. There was no time to waste; the daughters would be married off as soon as suitable boys were found for them.

The Hussains were drawing in Durga with their warmth; her visits to them were becoming more and more frequent. Still glum and detached at her son's place, Durga felt concerned if the Hussains' chrysanthemums wilted or their cakes did not rise. Heaven knows why she felt responsible in the Hussains' home.

Fatima, who was all the time part of everything, yet withdrawn, thanked her for teaching the girls so many useful things. Durga loved talking with Fatima who spoke little but was a good listener. By now she knew all about Durga's splendid childhood and her wonderful, romantic married life. Durga wept as she recalled her well-done home in Chandernagar where the rats must have by now gnawed up the carpets. What difference did it make, though! With her husband gone it did not matter if the expensive paintings fell to termites or the garden went to weeds.

One winter afternoon when the young Hussains had all gone for a film, Fatima gave a clue to the lines of patient resignation on her face. They were sitting in the garden, knitting, when Durga asked Fatima how long it had been since Mr. Hussain died.

"Seven years. These children were very young then," said Fatima, stifling a sigh.

"You must have been shattered."

"It wasn't very easy even when he was alive."

Durga did not want to ask personal questions so she simply looked at Fatima expectantly.

"I was married very young. I have a son and daughter. These children you see are from Mr. Hussain's second wife."

"What do you mean by his "second wife's when you are still alive," said Durga hotly.

"I was alive even then when he brought his new bride home, saying she was a gift for me."

"You didn't throw her out?" said Durga, almost panting with rage.

"Our men are allowed four wives. He brought home only one."

Durga stared at Fatima in disbelief. How could Fatima be rational about a second wife! She remembered how left-out she used to feel when her mother-in law would come to stay with her. How could Mrs. Hussain tolerate...in the same house!

"Where is she now," asked Durga.

"She died of jaundice nine years after her marriage, leaving behind four young children. I brought up these poor things."

"And your own children, where are they?"

"My daughter's married. My son is doing business in America. He wants me to settle down with him. But I can't. Not until these children settle down."

"Do you not hate these children?" Durga persisted.

"It was not their fault that they came into this world. And now they have only me. Hussain Sa'ab left enough money, and there is the business too, but human beings need love, don't they? Besides, they are so good to me."

"You've had a difficult time," said Durga, half in anger, half in admiration.

"Yes it was difficult," said Mrs. Hussain, slowly. "But it is on these difficult paths that one meets Allah."

Durga wept. Fatima expressed regret that she had saddened her.

Durga went home thinking about these startling revelations. All evening she thought about Fatima. She tried to re-live her trauma. Anger welled up within her. But then she recalled Fatima's quiet and dignified demeanour in which there was no anger or bitterness. Then she thought of her own self – her impulsive actions and words.

"Incredible," she kept saying to herself.

Durga recalled the Bhagavad Gita verses that were read out to her after her husband's death. Lines from Chapter 12 were now haunting her:

"The man whose soul is the same for his enemies or his friends...this man is dear to me."

It was 10 PM. The Hussains would be at dinner, but that thought didn't stop Durga from crashing into their home. She confronted Mrs. Hussain with:

"You are a karmayogi. No violence prevails in you. You are a true Vaisnava."

Mrs. Hussain understood not one of these epithets. She put her hands on Durga's shoulders and said, "You yourself are so good, that is why you think so well of me."

When a worried Akshay entered the Hussains' dining room wondering why his mother had rushed out at that hour, he was puzzled to see the two women weeping on each others' shoulders.

ppp

2

Joey — A Novella

Nairobi

Every evening little Joey and her black Labrador pup would wait for Babba to get home from work. When he did, he would be stranded at the door by their tempestuous welcome. "Easy, easy," he would plead, laughing helplessly as the child leapt into his arms and the pup leapt to lick his face. Shahnaaz (Ammu) would hold the struggling pup and it was only then that he would be able to enter his home. The living room would be smelling of fresh snacks and there would be flowers in the vases. He would say: "I have come back to the best home a woman has ever created," at which Shahnaaz would hug him, triggering off a fresh round of stormy affection from the pup and the child.

Joey was troublesome with meals. Mammu had to bait her with stories – each morsel going in with each progression in the story. Mammu would soon exhaust her stock of sleeping princesses and intrusive bears while Joey would fix her eyes on her face, asking for more. Laughing in despair, Mammu would then tell stories that had no story:

"The monkey climbed the tree, ate a berry, and threw the seed into the river. An alligator swallowed the seed and soon in his stomach sprouted a tree that grew berries. Another monkey ate the fruit of this tree and threw the seed into the river. Another crocodile swallowed the seed and there sprouted....Another monkey......threw the seed into the river. The crocodile's wife swallowed......."

Joey would listen enrapt, her eyes transfixed, as if this was a most suspenseful story. On days when Babba had time – as on weekends – Joey would lie in his arms, snuggling against his warm chest. His arms were soft and cushioned and on his back were five little red cysts, like rubies, that Joey kept stock of: "One...two ....three ...four ....five." After this ritual the stories would then flow. There would be yells of jubilant laughter when the clever monkey outsmarted the wily alligator or when the clever crow outsmarted the cunning fox.

Babba too told a story that had no story. He would invite Mammu to listen. He called it "The Tale of Two Cities." Joey loved this story which was about two rivers, both "proud and unyielding," in which the grey river outsmarted the blue one. Joey knew this story by heart, especially the part about the egrets – proud egrets who treated the soldiers with disdain, for in the cantonments they " walked amongst soldiers' boots, making light of salutes and parades." It tickled her to think of soldiers being outsmarted by confident little egrets. The "Tale of Two Cities" ran thus:

"Two rivers clasp around Allahabad, almost encircling it on all sides. But for a clearing in the south-west, Allahabad could well pretend to be an island. All that happens in Allahabad happens within the fold of these rivers. Yet the city behaves as if there were no rivers. There is no boat –

talk, no fish-talk, no river- talk, except among the fishermen and the boatmen.

Two proud rivers, one grey, the other blue, meet reluctantly near the Fort. The grey river draws its lines, so does the blue one. Then, after some underwater compromise, they agree to flow eastwards, under the name of the grey one.

Allahabad is also the city of two cantonments – one Old, the other New. Sprawling cantonments lie on all sides of the city. But the city behaves as if the army does not exist. Young boys borrow no swagger from the officers, nor do young girls swoon over them. The cantonment sticks to itself, as if the city does not exist.

Allahabad is a city of birds, especially water-birds. They fly from one river-bank to another, from one cantonment to another, tasting worms and waters. Egrets are completely at ease in all the cantonments. They walk amongst soldiers' boots with the assurance of cats, making light of parades and salutes; soldiers in green uniform, egrets in white."

Joey, the insatiable, insisted on hearing the story of the other city, to where the two rivers flowed as one.

A Tale of Two Cities

"The two rivers merge as one and flow into Mirzapur across lush fields of maize, millet and rice, and finally emerge in a little town. This little town by the river is truly blessed, unlike Allahabad where the two rivers have created deep schisms, making it a city of communities and gossip. The Goddess who watches upon Mirzapur from yonder hill knits its residents – the Hindus, the Muslims, and the few British that have stayed on, into a quiet weave. Here friendships end only in death and married sons still live with their mothers. Allahabad has a mind, Mirzapur has more heart. Come the monsoons and the surrounding hills burst into rivulets, grass, and village fairs, where women dressed in red and yellow buy green bangles, bead-necklaces and silver anklets...."

Babba's voice broke and little Joey began to wonder why the happiness of that place should make Babba's eyes fill with mist.

"The story ends here. You may complete it someday," said he.

Mirzapur

The bungalow is more than a hundred and fifty years old. It belonged to one Mr. White, who was then the city magistrate. He loved Mirzapur so much that he asked to be buried there. His grave is still to be found near the well and was well looked after by the next owner, Gajendra Chandra, and after him, by his son, Mahendra. It was fenced out of the bungalow compound as it is inauspicious to have a grave within the premises. One of the bungalow's gardeners, bored with weeding, created a sensation one moonless night by lighting eleven mustard oil diyas on the grave. He explained that petitions to White Sahib had cured him of a certain disease. Then onwards, every moonless night, one found bags of rice, fruit, sweets, saris, and even bangles on the grave, as tokens of gratitude for all sorts of personal problems having been solved with the intercession of White Sahib.

It was the 20th of December, 1972. Mahendra and his wife Sumitra were content to be with their daughters, Molly and Simmi, and their younger son, Robin (the older son was to come later). All three had come down from Allahabad, where they were in college. It was Christmas-break for them, and they were looking forward to a dizzy spell of parties. The British had introduced Mirzapur to picnics and parties. There was to be one on the 22nd, at the Bungalow, for which the chrysanthemum pots had to be arranged in the verandah and the crockery had to be brought out and washed. Sumitra and Mahendra were upset that their older son, Cuckoo, would not be able to come for the party. Cuckoo was the pride of the family. He was only twenty six but was already Assistant Collector, Meerut. Liveried attendants rushed about to open doors for him and polish his boots, serve him meals and help him put on his coat. His wife, Mohini, came from a wealthy family and had impressed her husband with her pragmatic approach to life and her smart solutions to problems.

Cuckoo may have been the pride of the family but it was Robin who was the son after Mahendra's heart. He was empathetic, self-effacing, and courageous. At parties Mahendra stood out, well groomed and suave, but in private he was a nervous man. As a landowner, his life was fraught with anxiety; land grabbers, trespassers, pests and predators kept him on his toes – to say nothing of sweating it out in courts against false claimants to his land. Cuckoo was too full of himself to help anybody; it was Robin who anticipated his problems and dealt with them. It miffed Cuckoo that the regard meant for the eldest son went to Robin, who was six years his junior.

There was much that Mahendra had taken care of. His mother had died when he was still an undergraduate, and his father followed her out of grief seven months later. Mahendra's brother, Raghav, who was ten years his junior, was still in school then, and there was a sister to marry off. What trouble he had from his sisters – Madhumalati and Sumangala! They were married into the wealthiest of families but they kept coming back to Mirzapur, would live there for months altogether, making life hell for Sumitra. But that is another story.

Mahendra's parents had left behind farmlands and bungalows. They had also left behind gold and silver and precious gems. The Chandras had kept some of this in the bank locker. The rest they hid under a stone slab in their bedroom, which they covered with a heavy wooden cupboard. Every four months, at night, when the servants were asleep, Mahendra and his wife would empty out the cupboard to push it aside. List in hand, they would check the hidden treasure. None of it was ill-gotten wealth; after India became independent and socialist, the income tax department kept an eye on people's assets. Even the land came under the Land Ceiling Act and had to be saved by registering excess land under the names of trusted friends and old family retainers. No one would dare betray Mahendra who had two very strong gun-trained sons: Priyavrata and Suvarna – Robin and Cuckoo.

Mahendra discontinued his studies after his father died and began farming his land for wheat, rice, and sugarcane. This took care of his expenses and Raghav's as well. The income helped him to keep comfortable all the overstaying married sisters, widowed aunts and parasitic uncles who occupied rooms in his large bungalow.

Mahendra's younger brother Raghavendra, better known as Raghav, had never shown any interest in the inheritance. His passion lay in machines; even as a child he had loved dismembering machines and reassembling them. He went on to study Mechanical Engineering at the Allahabad Engineering College. Soon after he got his engineering degree he married a Parsi girl, Shahnaaz, and moved to Africa to work for a company that manufactured electrical goods.

Crisis

It was the 21 st of December, 1972. In the kitchen the cook was stirring gajar ka halwa while his assistant was preparing matar ki kachauri. Simmi and Molly were practising a song that they were to present at the party the following day; Mahendra and Sumitra were deciding upon the dessert. Robin was setting up the drinks and wine glasses in the dining room. There was a call....from Nairobi. Raghav's employer had called up to say that both Raghav and Shahnaaz had died on the spot, in a car collision. Their child was at a friend's place when this happened.

Robin and Mahendra left for Africa, on a special visa that was hurriedly arranged by Mahendra's friend who was in the diplomatic services.

On reaching Nairobi, Mahendra and Robin went straight to Mrs. Weston's place, where Joey was. They found a confused little girl of seven, subdued by loss. Mahendra broke down on seeing her. Robin took her in his arms. Joey did not cry. She looked at him the way abandoned dogs do when you offer them food. As she sat on Robin's lap Joey looked carefully at him. How much he resembled her handsome Babba! Robin hardly left her side. He told her about animals and places and sketched little cartoons to amuse her. Mrs. Weston, who had insisted on hosting Mahendra and Robin, was relieved to see that there were people who would love little Joey. Though she was in her late fifties she had been close to the young and pretty Shahnaaz and the good-natured Raghav.

Meanwhile, in Mirzapur, Cuckoo had come home with his wife, Mohini. Sumitra was resentful that the unfortunate accident had cast a shadow over Cuckoo's holiday. He was the son after her heart, with whom she could share all resentments against Mahendra's intrusive relatives. Cuckoo was bitterly disappointed that the family would not be attending any of the parties they had been invited for, and instead of picnics there would be forced mourning. Sumitra, disgruntled for other reasons as well, launched into a discussion:

"Your grandfather died while Raghav was still in school. We took care of his education. Your father sacrificed his higher studies to take care of the farms and fields while Raghav studied. Not once did that boy make a round of the farm to help his brother! On the contrary, he went ahead to marry that Parsi girl who did not blend with us, and she took him away to Africa. And now we have to take care of his orphaned daughter. Is it a simple thing in India to take on the responsibility of a girl- child ! You first educate her, then get her married, and then lifelong you have to appease her husband's family with gifts and hospitality. The Parsis won't lift a finger for this child. They migrated to Australia soon after their daughter married Raghav. After all that we shall do for her, this child shall grow up and claim her father's property, forgetting all the expenditure incurred on her upbringing."

"Not just that, she will sell off her farms adjoining ours to strangers, who shall intrude into our fields and trouble us," added Cuckoo.

"Why even let her know about her property," suggested Cuckoo's wife, Mohini. "People will tell her, even if we don't," said Simmi.

"She's going to be a terrible nuisance," said Molly.

"We'll not let her know... we'll tell her that her father sold the property to us before he went to

Africa; which we are farming now," said Mohini.

"Mohini is simply brilliant," they chorused, thumping her on the back. Mohini had a nice smile, and nice hands, on which she wore beautiful rings – diamonds and emeralds, blue sapphire.

"Were it not for us, Raghav Uncle would have lost his property to the land mafia. He could not even hold a gun, leave alone use it," Cuckoo chuckled contemptuously. Sumitra pressed yet another point:

"She'll claim her jewels too." Mohini flashed a smile:

"We'll say it was all burgled." And there was another round of applause for Mohini.

"In any case, "said Cuckoo, "We should not allow her too much into our home."

"You have ideas!" said Sumitra."All my life I have housed some relative or the other from your father's side. Just let that kid come and you shall see how we shall have to dance around her."

Joey comes to Mirzapur

On the way to Mirzapur Robin told Joey: "In Mirzapur you shall meet one striped cat one brown dog and four cows.... How many animals does that make...?"

Joey caught the rhythm of Babba's storytelling voice in Robin's voice. The pain of leaving home was softened by his gentle eyes and his little attentions. On reaching Mirzapur, Joey was intimidated by the large bungalow and the coldness with which she was greeted. She clung to Robin in fear, but he said there was nothing to fear, they were all family.

Joey was told to address Sumitra as Badi Amma. There was no welcome in Badi Amma's eyes; Simmi and Molly looked at Joey with scorn. Sumitra wanted to put up Joey in the corner room where the bed- linen and towels were stored, but Robin put his foot down. He insisted that Joey sleep in the bedroom adjoining his parents' one, and that Gaumukhi, the kitchen assistant, should sleep in her room.

Gaumukhi was a brahmin widow who had served the family for decades. Now fifty, Goumukhi had lost her husband when she was eighteen. She had served Mahendra's mother, and had looked after the children, especially Raghav.

Joey was given a bed to sleep on; Gaumukhi slept on a carpet. At night Joey would snuggle close to Gaumukhi who would tell her about the wild animals in the jungles of Mirzapur: leopards, pythons, wild boar. She also told her about the inauspicious owl in whose presence names were not to be mentioned, for if it called out the name of a person, that person would die.

Gaumukhi also told her stories from the Ramayana. According to Gaumukhi, Robin reminded her of Lakshman because he was as devoted to Mahendra as Lakshman was to Ram.

School

There were no good schools in Mirzapur; the wealthy of the town usually sent their children to school in Allahabad. Allahabad was known for its educational institutions: the schools, the colleges, the famous University which was established by the British. During the British Raj, Christian missionaries came from Europe to set up some of the finest schools in the country.

Allahabad breathed grandeur; majestic churches and cathedrals, bungalows and gardens stood all over the city. The University, which was an architectural marvel, was a place for intellectual excellence. In the Company Garden the British had created a thing of beauty that would enchant forever; its unhappy history was forgotten and only the lush greenery remained. The Raj had, perhaps inadvertently, given back to the city much of what it had taken from the natives.

It was decided to send Joey to Santa Maria Girls' High School in Allahabad; Robin, who had enrolled in the University, would be supervising her studies. Mahendra and Robin took Joey to school for admission. The admissions were being looked after by the Vice Principal, Mrs. Wallace. She turned down Joey firmly when she came to know about her orphan status: "We have admitted such children in the past, and when the child is in trouble the relatives do not turn up," she said decisively.

Mahendra was disheartened; Robin suggested that they meet the Principal Mrs. Hayer. Mrs. Hayer inducted Joey into the school amid Mrs. Wallace's protests; Joey would live in the Lady Fatima wing of the hostel. Mrs. Wallace never forgave Joey this slight.

School: Problems and their Resolution

A nervous Joey was taken to the hostel by a young and firm, though kindly Miss. Pratt. In the dormitories the girls were laughing and talking at the top of their voices. Some were throwing pillows at each other while some were kicking an imaginary football. Miss Pratt asked the girls to take care of Joey, and left. One of the Class Eight girls walked towards Joey with a swagger.

"I say, who is this little insect who has joined mid-session?"

She had big, bright eyes and her hair fell to her forehead in a fashionable fringe. A gang of four followed her wherever she went. She sized up Joey and asked, "So...what is your name?"

"My name is Yashodhara," mumbled Joey, looking down.

"Whattt !!!,"said Big Eyes,.

"My name is Yashodhara," repeated Joey.

Big Eyes looked at the others in mock confusion.

"Is that a name?"

Joey kept looking at her shoes.

"What can it mean?" said the one with slanting eyes.

"Yashodhara was Lord Buddha's wife," said Joey.

At this they all yelled and laughed. The wife part tickled them very much. Helpless with laughter, Big Eyes said," She's Lord Buddha's wife, so she's our great, great, great grandmother."

"We'll call you Granny... right?"said Pink Lips. Pink Lips was expelled by the school two years later for her graffiti on the bathroom walls. She had written "bastardine" all over, and had also drawn some objectionable diagrams of the human anatomy.

"What does your father do?" asked the one with the broad waist.

"He's an engineer," said Joey, almost sobbing.

"Why are you crying, you sissy? jeered Round Eyes.

"She's watering the garden," said another girl.

"And now we shall grow pumpkins," said yet another "We shall have pumpkin-pie to eat."

"Ask her to show her navel" said Pink Lips to Round Eyes, who decided to keep that for another time. She asked instead:

"And where are you from?"

Joey decided not to answer any more.

"All right just answer this one for today and we'll let you go," assured Round Eyes: "Where do you come from?"

"Africa," mumbled Joe. They all yelled in a chorus:

"Affricca ....of all places....!! Affricca!!. Oh my God!!!,"and they laughed till their sides hurt.

Mrs. Pratt, who was making her rounds appeared suddenly.

"What are you doing here .... And why is this girl crying?"

"Ma'am we were merely asking her name," said Round Eyes.

"Don't you bully this child – she is an orphan," admonished Miss. Pratt.

Miss Pratt meant well but did not know how to do it well. News of Joey's orphanhood spread fast, and soon all in the school knew about it. Joey now knew that she was a species apart.

Robin's Visit and its Consequences

The school allowed the local guardians to meet their hostel wards only on fixed days, for a fixed time. Mahendra had requested the Principal to allow Robin to look up Joey more often than was the rule. So within a few days he came to meet her during lunch-break. It was a bright winter day and all looked fresh under a deep blue sky. The girls, big and small, were out in the fields, and they saw a pleasant young man comfort a little girl and even succeed in making her smile. He looked handsome under the bright sunshine. The senior school girls noticed his confident bearing, his hair, his smile. Robin's appearance in school altered the weather for Joey; the senior school girls now took it upon themselves to take care of her wellbeing. In between straightening her tie and tidying up her hair they would, with studied indifference, ask about her cousin – who he was and what he did.

The Sports Captain of Santa Maria, Anita Pandey, was also the Head Girl of the Lady Fatima wing of the hostel. The junior school had a massive crush on her; the girls hung about in places where they might possibly get a glimpse of her. She was the star athlete of the school; she was simply majestic. No one as self-assured and stunning had ever come to Santa Maria. The girls adored her from a distance – she was too stately to be approached.

Anita began to show a keen interest in Joey's emotional and physical wellbeing. She loved to hear Robin's name over and over again, and there was nothing better that Joey liked than to talk about the cousin she adored. Anita's attentions did change Joey's status from "African orphan" to "Anita's darling" but it aroused Round Eyes' jealousy towards her, and we all know how harmful a jealous person can be.

Round Eyes kept devising ways to trouble Joey in some way or the other. Joey was wretched until she found a new source of comfort: the school chapel. She would make desperate prayers to Mary: "Mother, I have not stolen Round Eyes' paint- box, but she is saying that I have. She and her friends always make fun of me....Mother, don't punish her, but do protect me from her..."

When the going was rough and the day was bleak – which would be mostly so for an orphan, Joey sought refuge in daydreaming. She would dream of black puppies licking her cheeks; she would dream of bright nasturtiums; but most of the time she would dream of Robin telling all the girls in school how much he loved his little sister, Joey.

Reports of Joey's inattentiveness in class, of her constant daydreaming, reached Mahendra. Joey's report cards were a disgrace. It was over two years since she had joined Santa Maria but she remained steadily at the bottom of the class. Mahendra began to feel that he was letting down his deceased brother, a matter he confided in Robin. Robin went to the Principal and asked to be permitted to teach Joey for just four Saturdays. It was also decided that Robin, and not Mahendra, would now be signing her report card.

Robin began looking into Joey's studies. Every Saturday the Principal would have her chamber opened for him. Suddenly for Joey, Mathematics became more interesting and History more meaningful. Everything that Robin touched turned to gold.

The teachers were amazed at the improvement; Joey wanted Robin to sign a decent report-card.

Vacations in Mirzapur

The summer vacations used to be more than two months long. Mahendra would come in his deep blue Ambassador, number ending 8888, to take her home. He saw to it that something special was cooked for Joey as long as she was in Mirzapur. He would play Ludo, and Snakes and Ladders with her and show her his childhood photographs. She liked it best when he took her into the garden and introduced her to all sorts of plants and trees: the majestic mahua, the umbrageous pakar, the stately ashok....

In the evenings Joey would steal into the servants' quarters where Gaumukhi would feed her "village rotis" and aloo bharta. In the servants' quarters also lived the loquacious Mohammed Karim, the "Attendant of

Machines," which covered all dysfunctional things, be they cars or leaking taps or broken window panes. His father, Mustafa, had served the Bungalow for thirty years, in the very same capacity. Karim's mother had died when he was eight and, henceforth, he followed his father everywhere, preparing to step into his shoes – now handing him the screws, now the hammer. The servants' quarters admired Mustafa for his quiet patience, his steadiness. His loyalty to the master became the model for the rest of the servants to follow. They also admired him for not thrusting a step-mother upon his child when his wife died. Mustafa was only thirty four when that happened, and the servants' quarters had stepped in to bathe and feed Karim by turns. Gaumukhi had grabbed the role of foster mother, and a strong bond emerged between her and Karim which expressed itself through constant bickering.

When Karim was twenty Mustafa succumbed to renal failure. The grieving Karim went into a long and sullen silence that irked Gaumukhi. She always became restive when he gave up on food, for food was the cord between him and her. The month- long fast during Ramzan always threatened to loosen this cord; she would create such tantrums that Karim would yield to her and fast only on the first and last days of Ramzan. After Mustafa's death she became desperate and addressed Public Opinion:

"I have brought this boy up ....can a single morsel go down my throat when this fellow stops eating? As for people of his caste, they are trained to go hungry and thirsty for months altogether, but me, I am not trained to go hungry....see how my stomach has caved in."

The mention of Ramzan infuriated Karim: "Never has this woman allowed me to observe my fast in peace. You see the result ? My father too has died because I could never fast during Ramzan,"he told Public Opinion.

"Had it been so, your Allah would have killed me and not your father, and t'were good had He done so. Is there anyone more unfortunate than I am? I became a widow in my youth, spent all my energies and resources on this fellow, who is now starving me to death." Much to Karim's embarrassment, she exposed her stomach before all the people in the servants' quarters, even the men. Her tamasha was more unbearable than his father's death. He decided to return to normal, which meant eating and bickering.

The sight of Gaumukhi smoking a beedi brought out the worst in Karim. But even before he could tell her how shameful it was that a brahmin, a widow, should smoke like a gypsy, she would start accusing him of having stolen her beedies. He would retort: "If I had to steal would steal the malik's Mulboro (Marlborough) cigarettes. He would raise his voice for all to hear: "I buy her beedies, with my money, and she accuses me of stealing them!." He never mentioned the saris he bought her. He had even persuaded her to stop wearing "widow white."

"What a society!!! A woman loses her husband at eighteen and she goes through life alone, scrubbing other people's floors, wearing white."

"It's better to wear white than to live with three other wives," Gaumukhi retorted.

"Ah Bibi, (she was Amma when he was hungry, and Bibi when quarelling) don't make me open my mouth about the third wife sending the first wife's son to the jungle for fourteen years!!!....and if you weren't such a wretched old woman I would tell you about a man having sixteen thousand wives, in a certain society."

"You orphan, you would have been in your grave by now, had I not fed you"......They would go on, all day. But they could not live without each other.

Karim spiced up the lives of the servants with his "experiences." Most of them were set in the Vindhyan hills. The timing would invariably be 2 AM. Stories of groans arising from abandoned wells; stories of cobras waylaying him as he sauntered through the hills; of pythons falling from trees, crushing him under their weight for several hours; had the python not moved in pursuit of a deer, he would have died of suffocation. On several occasions jinns had stopped him to ask him for a beedi. Such was the grip of his narrative that no one wondered why he roamed the hills after midnight. Back in her room, Joey would recall his tales and feel frightened. She would cling to Gaumukhi who would calm her: "Don't you believe a word of what he says – that Karim is a born liar. That liar wakes me up at midnight because he's scared to go to the toilet alone in the dark."

He indeed was. One had to cross the orchard to use the toilet, and the banana tree, with its leaves torn by the wind, frightened him the most. Even the moon frightened him for looking upon him – nay, it singled him out to peer upon. When Gaumukhi would trace his fears to his irrational belief in jinns and jinnats, Karim would hiss back that she disliked jinns and jinnats because they were Muslim spirits, and that she was only an old, ignorant, fanatic, brahmin widow.

Vacations in Mirzapur (Continued)

Exams gave over. Soon it would be time for the summer break. Despite Badi Amma, Joey looked forward to the vacations, for it would be summer break for Robin as well. And he would take out the car after the first shower of rain and drive the family to the Wyndham Falls. The Falls gushed down a long stretch of rocks which were smooth with age, fine-terraced by water. They were dark and ancient. The way to Wyndham was through the hills, wild, uninhabited, with the silence of what Wordsworth called, "The souls of lonely places."

The place that Joey loved most, however, was not Wyndham but Barr Ghat, where a shallow stream flowed through rocks, a stream so shallow in places that it made puddles, with fish in it, and wild lilies grew between rocks. If you went there on a March morning you would see kingfishers wearing white cravats, and kingfishers with brown cravats, swoop sharp into the water and come out neat, with fish in mouth. And in March you would find a tree laden with white blooms and bees. This was the place that persistently barged into her daydreams.

On the way back from Barr Ghat, they would stop at Madhiyan for gulab jamuns and chai. In the winter-break Robin would organize boat rides down the Ganga. Six families would get together and go down the Ganga under the blue sky, carrying the best that they could cook. Robin would point out Gregory Sahib's kothi to Joey, which the locals managed to pronounce as Gargaria Sahib ki kothi. The face of the bungalow was intact but the rear portion was in ruins. It was the most romantic thing that Joey had ever seen, apart from the ancient ruins of a temple in the woods. Mirzapur was countless romance: the woods, the rivulets, the gracious lives of the wealthy. A wealthy diaspora lived quietly among the woods and villages – the British who owned and ran the carpet industry in that region. The British of Mirzapur reminded Joey of her parents' British friends in Africa, who, like those in Mirzapur, she associated with tasteful homes and gardens, and muffins and mince-pies. During Christmas they hosted lavish dinners and tea-parties. Mirzapur looked forward to Edgar Russel's grand Christmas party. Joey looked forward to the flambé that the chef would carry in with panache; the cake made a grand entry, like royalty, everyone looking at it in silent applause.

However, everywhere, in all seasons, it was Robin who was the Prince of Hearts, ensuring peace and comfort to all, and no place, not even Barr Ghat would be as good as it felt, without him.

Mammu and Babba Wedding

It was a winter morning. Joey looked out of the dormitory window. Heavy dew lay on everything. It subdued the green of the grass and made the leaves look pale. In the light of the morning sun, dewdrops shone on nasturtium leaves like quicksilver. The skies were a crisp blue. Winter in Allahabad was just as beautiful as Mammu used to describe it.

Like Mammu, Joey grew up to be a nature addict, a bird addict, a sky addict. She walked this world with her thoughts in another; the other world was one in which kingfishers posed proudly against the sky, and parrots swung by the ears of corn. This world was demanding of urgent attention – if you were slack, the morning-glory would retreat unto itself, unnoticed; if you heeded not, the moon would sink beyond the trees, lonely and disappointed. Joey, the daughter of Shahnaaz – the daughter of Firoze and Shireen Batliwala, knew of every leaf in the garden, and every fallen feather.

Batliwala ran one of the most famous book-stores in Northern India, called Pages. Allahabad was an intellectual city and book-lovers came to it from neighbouring cities looking for books they could not find elsewhere. Batliboy earned well and could indulge in expensive hobbies, like collecting vintage cars, and was probably the inspiration behind the vintage car rallies that were flagged off from Polo Ground every December.

Batliwala's bookstore gave him wealth in the form of friendship as well; it was in Pages that he met VK Joshi. Joshi was a professor in the Allahabad University and a regular customer to his shop. From Joshi's taste in books you could never guess the subject he taught – he bought books on astrology, philosophy, homeopathy, birds, gardening, poetry. He was a professor of mathematics.

Batliwala and Joshi would sit in the Coffee House every evening, discussing books and politics. They became such good friends that they decided to build their homes next to each other's, no fences dividing them.

Batliwala was tall and composed. The cigarette between his fingers solved all problems. Joshi was, short, plump and excitable. When he read a novel you could somewhat guess what he was reading from the way he said, "Bastard," or "Maaro saaley ko." If the novel ended on a happy note he would go into the kitchen and hug his wife, if not, he would go on an unscheduled walk.

Joshi was Mahendra's schoolmate. When Raghav went to school in Allahabad, and lived in a hostel, Joshi became his local guardian. By the time he reached college, Raghav had become indispensable in the Joshi household. In Joshi's home anything amiss, be it a fuse blown out, or a punctured tyre, was a calamity at par with the Great Flood. Nor could Joshi handle the servants, who were always out of hand. They would borrow big amounts of money from him and vanish for months altogether. Raghav began handling Joshi's difficulties.

Joshi's own son, Vaidurya, had inherited his father's mathematical genius and had gone to the USA on a scholarship when he was sixteen. He took up American citizenship for he was not comfortable in India anymore.

It was in Joshi's house that Raghav met Shahnaaz. A confidence sprung up between them; he wouldn't feel at ease until he had told her all: the runs he made in the cricket-match; the professor who had marked him down unfairly; the kind of language his classmates used; she even knew of his infatuation with Shiela Fernandes. It was mostly a monologue, for Shahnaaz was a quiet girl. And so serene that you would feel peaceful by merely being in her presence.

Raghav had just completed the engineering course and would now be applying for a job. But before that he decided to take a short break by going for a thirteen day trek on the Western Ghats. The trek turned out to be more adventurous than he had imagined, and he was now keen to rush to Allahabad to tell Shahnaaz all about it the ridges he had crossed, the animals he had encountered, and the ineffable silence of the hills at dawn. The hills were cut off from all habitation and all technology, else he would have phoned her every single day to tell her all his experiences.

When Raghav returned to Allahabad he found the homes of the Joshis and the Batliwalas in a state of high activity; Batliwala's home was being decorated with flowers and fairy lights; streamers of marigold were hung all over the verandahs and the pathway was strewn with rose petals. A strong aroma of spices could be caught from far off.

"Shahnaaz is getting engaged," answered Joshi.

Raghav went behind the little temple in the tobacco field and wept.

The time for the engagement was drawing close. Even the normally composed Batliwala was a flustered man this afternoon. Both he and Joshi were barking last-minute instructions to the staff. The boy's people were coming down all the way from Sri Lanka where they owned tea estates. They were extremely wealthy. The boy, Navroze, had been suggested by Batliwala's cousin. Navroze had seen Shahnaaz's photo. He had had a couple of conversations with her on phone and had liked her very much – enough to book tickets right away, for the engagement. It all happened within ten days.

Back in Batliwala's house, Raghav said not a word.He clung to Batliwala and wept. Shahnaaz, who stood radiant in fuschia pink, went pale and clung to the sobbing Raghav. Looks were exchanged between Joshi and Batliwala. Batliwala made a quick decision. A rattled Mrs. Batliwala shook Shahnaaz by the shoulders, asking if she too wanted Raghav.

Navroze Reshamwala, the groom-to-be, had flown down with twenty friends and family members – all the way from Sri Lanka. The entire Parsi community of Allahabad had been invited, along with other friends of Batliwala. Batliwala's son too had flown down from Australia for the occasion. All eyes were on the handsome groom-to-be, who was all aglow with love and joy.

The Reshamwallahas were disappointed but gracious. They insisted that the engagement ceremony between Rahgav and Shahnaaz be performed as per schedule. Batliwala, as if paralysed with guilt and confusion, slumped into a chair. The Reshamwallahs initiated the engagement. Raghav wept all through the ceremony, overwhelmed with mixed feelings. But in Shahnaaz's heart there was calm, and the peace of fulfillment that comes from having found true love.

The guests were confused.Several Parsis walked out. Those who stayed back made grim faces. They did not hide their feelings about the handsome and rich Parsi boy, who looked so dashing in a blue suit, and the usurping non-Parsi who looked pale and tired. "Selfish boy."

"Selfish girl – what low behavior on her part towards people who had traveled all the distance from Sri Lanka. And as for Feroze and Shireen Batliwala, the less said of them the better: This comes of hanging out too much with non-Parsis. Could he have not made a home away from the Joshis?" The Parsis would never forgive Batliwala his betrayal of a good Parsi who had traveled a long way to marry his daughter.The Shahnaaz-Raghav wedding was a small affair boycotted, of course, by the Parsis.

Raghav brought his bride home to Mirzapur where Mahendra threw a lavish party. Mirzapur raved over the bride, "What a lovely smile the bride has, and such a gentle and serene face...." Mahendra and Raghav's sisters, Madhumalati and Sumangala, were married into royalty. All they did all day was to change their hairdos and match their jewellery with their saris. But the dour expression on their faces always remained the same. At parties their voices were heard the loudest, flirting, drawing attention, throwing baits like: "I am seasoned wood, I am old wine." Sumangala and Madhumalati tore Shahnaaz to pieces, in voices loud enough for her to hear. They called Batliwala a petty businessman selling a petty product. "Huh!! Books!!"Surely, Shahnaaz had hooked Raghav for his property, they said. They went on to make fun of the way Parsis dressed, and the way they spoke.

Gaumukhi took Raghav aside and told him not to leave his bride alone with the women of the family. She also advised him to stay away from Mirzapur.

Batliwala, heartbroken due to the attitude of his community, decided to go away to his son in Australia. Shahnaaz began to stay sad over these repercussions of her marriage. Joshi advised Raghav to work outside India. Raghav seized the first job that he got – in Nairobi, where he and Shahnaaz set up a beautiful home and had a lovely child, whom Mrs. Weston decided to call Joey. Mrs. Weston stood by Shahnaaz all through her pregnancy and childbirth.

The Joshis and Joey

After Batliwala left India Joshi was heartbroken and began to keep uncertain health. "My son is settled abroad, my friends are gone, what do I have left in life?" he would say. His wife, Gita, would remind him of Joey, who was their responsibility as well. Joey felt at home in their place and addressed them as Nana and Nanu.

Badi Amma was cold as ever and Robin had become distant ever since Joey grew up. The Joshis made her feel loved and wanted.

Robin Gets a Job and Prepares to Leave

There was much excitement and celebration in Mirzapur. Robin had qualified for the prestigious Indian Foreign Service. Mahendra's heart burst with pride to think of Robin negotiating as ambassador, with England.... France.... America.... He threw a lavish party to celebrate, for which relatives came from far and stayed a week; all the servants and their children were given new clothes, and Gaumukhi was at last gifted the silver necklace of her desire.

The servants'quarters was unanimous in the conclusion that good karma always pays off, that Robin had earned his success due to his filial devotion, that he was a prince not only in looks but also at heart.

Joey came down to Mirzapur to meet Robin before he left for training. Her heart sank at the very thought of his departure. He would be leaving late in the evening, on the 28th of April.

On the 28th Mahendra was restless. All sorts of anxieties crossed his mind. Robin was the son he had relied upon ... how would he manage the farm without him? Mahendra was not one to complain, but as the time drew close for Robin to leave, regrets from the past trudged through his mind. Ever since he was nineteen, when his father died, he had borne the burden of the family with grit and grace. The overstaying uncles and widowed aunts had said unkind things to him and his wife, but he had never reacted. The land-mafia, the house grabbing tenants made him run from one court to another, from the police to the magistrates.......He had worked in heat and rain, amidst cobras and pythons; the standing crops would be destroyed by unseasonal rain, or hailstorm .... He worked hard to keep his sisters' husbands appeased. As the older son he had had to attend all the funerals; in that large family somebody or the other kept dying; how he hated the wailing of the families, how he hated the long rituals before the body was consigned to fire! ....His older son, the district magistrate, had eyes only for his wife; he visited his parents less and her parents more....and when he came home he either praised himself or her parents, never asking how his father kept up appearances when the crops failed – which was ever so often!

Robin wanted to spend the last one hour with his father. An unspoken sadness hung between, them. Robin too was thinking of the land mafia and house -grabbing tenants. His elder brother cared only for his wife's family …. ever since Cuckoo had got married all one heard from him was how smoothly his wife's family lived, how wealthy they were, and what expensive gifts they gave him.

Robin dreaded the time when he would be posted abroad and his father would go from one court to another….his father looked so old today….he noticed bags under his eyes. This very man used to be the life of every party, the best gunshot in town, brought up by English governesses, trained in the delicacies of etiquette….

A few minutes before Robin was to leave, Mahendra went to the toilet. On his way back he fell with a loud thud. Robin rushed in and saw his father on the floor, holding his heart, writhing in pain. The doctors later cautioned Robin that there should be no recurrence of the attack.

It did not take Robin too long to decide. Under no circumstances would he leave his father. He told Mahendra about this only when he was quite recovered.

"I am not going anywhere, I am going to take care of everything. Everything," he told his weeping father.

Mahendra broke into sobs, "I don't want you to be a farmer. I want you to be an ambassador to England, to France."

"Such middle-class nonsense you are talking, Dad. You know I love farming, and that is that." This is how Robin became man of the house, looking after the farms, the taxes, the litigations….and of course the visiting relatives. He surprised his father one day by announcing his plans to set up a brewery on a piece of land just adjacent to his farm.

"Do you not think this would be a big strain on him....the farm is big enough," Mahendra said to his wife.

"That boy has so much energy in him, he could set up five such breweries and not be tired, "said Sumitra, who was not a worrier like her husband.

Robin gets Married

Mahendra and Sumitra had gone to Bombay to attend a wedding where they were introduced to Mr. and Mrs. Kumar. Mr. Kumar was an industrialist. Mahendra was greatly affected by Mr. Kumar's suave manner and his wife's grace. Mr. Kumar invited Mahendra and Sumitra home for tea. Sumitra and Mahendra were impressed with the size of Kumar's bar and the beauty of his house. They also met their daughter, Lavani. Lavani was extraordinarily attractive. Even Sumitra could not take her eyes off her.

Sumitra and Mahendra believed that marriage should be socially enhancing; Mahendra's favourite quote was that it is better for a man to marry above his station and walk humbly ever after than to marry below his station and feel the embarrassment of having done so. They had chosen well for their elder son, a wife whose family had the same compulsions to hide gold and silver underground as they themselves had. Mohini's parents had gone a step further in burying part of their treasure under the guava tree in the inner courtyard.

On their return from Bombay, Mahendra received a phone-call from Mr.Kumar: he had liked the Chandras so much that he would be honoured if they would accept Lavani as their daughter-in-law. Mahendra and Sumitra were delighted.

The proposal was put before Robin who was too busy and irritable to pay attention to it. Day in and day out Mahendra and Sumitra kept persuading him to meet the girl. Robin said firmly that he would not go around "seeing" girls and rejecting them; if his parents liked the girl it was alright with him, though he was not prepared for marriage yet. Gentle reader, do not be shocked, most arranged marriages happened those days in India without the boy and the girl meeting each other.

The wedding was fixed for the 25 th of Nov. Joey would travel with the marriage party to Bombay. This was the first family wedding she would be attending, and she was excited.

All the cousins had gathered for the wedding. Joey had never imagined how much fun a wedding could be. Everything seemed aplenty – music, dance, flowers; the fragrance of marigold and roses mingled with French perfumes; there was endless food and endless laughter. The young and old were teased alike. Such a stream of joy and laughter: an Indian wedding.

Sixty people from the groom's side would be traveling to Bombay where they would be pampered silly by the bride's people. It was indeed a fairytale wedding – the groom so handsome and the bride so pretty, and the place all adazzle with flowers and glitter. Women in red and pink and green and yellow Kanjivaram and Banarasi saris, laden with jewelry, and the men all dapper in blue and black suits.

Robin saw his bride for the first time when the ceremonies began. She took his breath away. The following morning the groom's family reached the Kumars' home to take the bride away. Lavani was getting ready while the wedding party had breakfast. Joey went through one of the bedrooms to use the toilet. She was set to come out when she heard angry voices in the bedroom. Lavani had entered the room, banging the door behind her, followed by her equally furious mother. Joey heard Lavani tell her mother: "You wanted me to get married, so I have got married....and now you stay out of my life....stop telling me who to meet and who not to meet."

"You horrible girl, you shall not meet Raj Abhishek anymore. Do you understand?"

"Why should I not meet him? You did what you wanted to and I shall now do what I want to."

"Don't you dare meet that low-class bounder."

"I will meet him, and let's see what you can do about it."

Joey was sixteen, and old enough to realise the kind of life that lay ahead for Robin. The bedroom scene being over, a smiling Mrs.Kumar and an equally smileful Lavani met the groom's party. Joey was full of loathing. It made her angry to see Robin look at Lavani with love and longing. Young though she was, she knew she must keep what she knew, to herself.

The bride was given a princess's welcome in Mirzapur. Flower petals were showered upon her as she entered the house, stepping on a pathway made of rose petals. Lavani was all smiles, touching the feet of the elders, caressing the cheeks of the children. The house was full of fragrance .... of tuberoses, wild roses, marigold... Robin's room had been decorated with flowers for the wedding night: white silken sheets strewn with rose petals; rich red and gold cushions to go with the equally rich red and blue carpet.

The morning after, Lavani was full of smiles but Robin looked restless. He even left the guests and went to the farm on the pretext of an emergent situation. It would be the same, every morning at breakfast – Robin snapping at people, making cynical remarks, leaving in a huff.

Mahendra and Sumitra began to feel apprehensive. Mahendra began to blame himself, that he had pushed Robin into marriage. Neither he nor Sumitra had the courage to ask Robin what the matter was.

Lavani, meanwhile, made it out as if she was putting on a brave front. A fortnight after the wedding she broke into tears and said to Mahendra and Sumitra: "I don't think he likes me....I think he was interested in some other girl....he does not allow me to even come close to him....he has never once touched me."

When Mahendra and Sumitra finally took Robin aside, asking if anything was the matter with him, he exploded: "You asked me to marry this girl, and I did. And now you stay out of my personal matters."

Lavani complained that she found Robin crude and coarse," I feel uncomfortable being alone with him....I wish to go back home."

Lavani was so genteel in her behavior that the Chandras began to doubt their son who was, no doubt, showing signs of aggression ever since the wedding night. Mahendra said, sighing heavily, "We raised our son to be a decent man, but one can never say how a man is going to behave with a woman in private."

Mahendra phoned up the Kumars and suggested that it would be good if Lavani spent some time in Bombay, "She seems homesick." But the Kumars would have none of it.

"She's a silly, immature girl. With such a fine husband why should she be homesick! It's all our fault, we were too conservative; she went to an all-girls' school and has never been exposed to men. She should stay right there, she'll soon be fine," said Mrs. Kumar.

Heartbreak for Robin

Three years later, Robin sat glass in hand, cursing his inability to get drunk. There was so much to forget....the days passed in work, but the evenings were unbearable. When he sat alone the memories of his wedding night would erupt: his bride, dressed in pink....he feeling helpless before her beauty; the heady fragrance of rose and jasmine; he had sat before her, knowing not what to say. He could have looked at her for hours, days, so beautiful she was.

He had stretched out his hand awkwardly towards her. She had withheld hers, perhaps out of shyness, he had thought. Her mesmerizing beauty and the silence of that expectant moment were shattered by her unbelievable words: "You do not fit into my picture of a husband....I do not wish to begin any relationship with you."

He had gone numb with disbelief. He had rationalized her words as her inability to accept a change of place and situation. He gently asked her if somebody from his family had offended her. She said she hated herself for succumbing to parental pressure – he was not the sort of man she would have liked to spend her life with. And that was final.

The firmness in her voice left him with little doubt. Still he said, "Surely you are hurt about something. I shall try to give you my best... I can only plead before you that my family should not get to know your feelings about me ....my father has a heart problem."

He had slept on the carpet, and she on the bed. In the morning he put the pillow and quilt back on the bed, as if he had slept on it. And he did so, night after night.

He recalled the morning following that heartbreaking night; he had given it out to his parents that a crisis had come up on the farm and that he would remain both vexed and busy for quite a while. He would often skip breakfast and have tea and biscuits on the way to the farm, while his parents would wait for him to join them. Every morning Lavani would look her best at the breakfast table, perfumed and radiant, while he would be snapping at everyone, finding fault with the food and the upkeep of the house. The very servants who had adored him now began to dread him – with the exception of Ram Sevak and Gaumukhi.

He hated himself, for even three years after that terrible night he was still his wife's prisoner. All these three years she had kept coming in and going out of Mirzapur. It was such a relief when she was not there. His own mother had started playing into Lavani's hands and often spoke against him. Even the servants were enamoured of Lavani – all except Gaumukhi and Ram Sevak. Like Gaumukhi, Ram Sevak had served in the Bungalow for generations.

Mystery Unravelled

Having lived all by herself since she was eighteen, Gaumukhi had developed high intuition. She could "smell" people, and something told her to keep a watch over Lavani's movements, and also over Veeru Thapa, the young Nepali boy who was besotted with Lavani. All these years Gaumukhi had done the dusting in Robin's bedroom, but when Lavani came she asked Thapa to do it, on the plea that Gaumukhi could not reach high window panes and cupboards.

Gaumukhi confided in Ram Sevak that Lavani was paying Thapa handsome amounts to post her letters. That was enough to alert Ram Sevak who was extremely loyal; besides, he had read the sadness in Robin's eyes. Thapa was the "tea and coffee boy" and was also the "pantry boy." Just when Thapa would be about to leave, to post the letters, Ram Sevak would assign him some urgent work.

Lavani would never post single envelopes. Several letters, addressed to her friends and cousins, and to one Raj Abhishek, would be posted every other day. Gaumukhi discovered where exactly Thapa hid the letters when there was any obstacle in posting them immediately. Ram Sevak would let go the letters that were addressed to other people, but he held back all letters addressed to one Raj Abhishek. If Thapa did notice that some envelopes were missing, he did not say so, for he was only interested in the money he was gaining from Lavani. Ram Sevak also held back letters that the postman brought from Raj Abhishek.

One day Ram Sevak went to Robin and handed him over the letters, saying that it looked like Thapa had forgotten to post them. The look in his eyes conveyed much to Robin; Robin's hands trembled as he opened the envelopes. Lavani had written to Raj:

"The joy of my life, it's been almost three weeks since I felt your flesh against mine...your exhilarating flesh. It's been so long since I looked into your eyes.... your eyes intoxicated with my beauty. So long since your warm hands touched me... No one can love me as you did.

The best you loved me was on the afternoon of my wedding day. Your passion, your energy, is still fresh upon my limbs. I do not wish to dilute that memory....I have not let this fellow I have married, touch me even once."

Another letter said:

"Promise me that you will marry me. Promise me that you will divorce your wife soon. Only when you do so can I chuck this husband of mine out of my life. My parents threaten not to support me if I leave this fellow. Such a place is India!! This is no country for women.

I am so miserable here. Mirzapur is like a village. Can you imagine, they keep cows and buffaloes in the backyard!! Cow-dung stinks! They grow silly old vegetables in the compound. And they keep telling me the names of silly old flowers. Who's interested in flowers? One can buy them in the market...."

Robin shut himself in the toilet. He turned on the tap and sobbed. The little hope of his marriage surviving had now collapsed.

While Lavani wrote to Raj everyday, sometimes even thrice a day, Raj was prudent about sending letters to Lavani. Raj's letters to Lavani were infrequent. Robin learnt how to open envelopes and paste them back. Having read several letters, he now decided to go to Allahabad to meet Jamal Ansari. Jamal Ansari was a leading lawyer in Allahabad and was one of Mahendra's most trusted friends.

Jamal heard Robin out. He was a man with a set expression which did not break even when he cracked a joke in that wry manner of his; but when he came to know of Robin's distress a mist came over his eyes. He brooded a while before he said: "See, young man, I will not advise a divorce; the Indian law, as it stands today, is loaded in favour of women. If you file a divorce suit your wife shall take away a good portion of your property and also your income from the factory. You shall become a pauper, and she will have a merry time. She may not even agree for a divorce, for it will be more convenient for her to continue having her flings with men while retaining the respectability of a married woman. The only ground on which divorce can be granted is adultery, the proof of which is difficult to acquire. I suggest that you don't make a noise about the letters. Keep reading them. Post some, keep some.

You never know when they may come in handy."

Robin kept abreast of Lavani's dalliances through the letters. Raj Abhishek's letters were brief and formal. He always made it a point to mention his wife. In one of his letters he wrote: ".......I have been worried for my wife. She has been unwell. Nothing serious, just aches and pains and fatigue. She just will not relax – she's quite a perfectionist."

Another letter said: "I have put on a lot of weight; my wife has joined cookery classes. She was always a fantastic cook; Lord why did she have to get even better! I will have to now extend my morning walks."

The absence of intimacy in Raj's letters was making Lavani desperate. She immediately had her tickets booked for Bombay. This was just four months after the wedding. While she packed her suitcase she stopped Robin who was in a tearing hurry for a meeting of the Board of Directors of the brewery:

"I shall leave and never come back. You shall repent the way you have treated me. You shall rot. Your parents shall rot." Robin was flabbergasted at the injustice of all she said, but kept silent.

He was immensely relieved when she left. Come back she did. Came and went, only to return and make life hell for him.

Raj Abhishek. Bombay

The Kumars were greatly distressed by Lavani's arrival in Bombay. They threatened her with dire consequences if she met Raj again.

Soon Lavani was in Raj's office. He ran a small business of automobile parts, but his office was plush and he himself was well-groomed. He had studiously cultivated the manner of a public school product and generally presented himself as a nice, clean-shaven, sophisticated guy.

Raj was surprised to see Lavani. He was surrounded by not-so-public school looking men and was negotiating some deal that nice guys wouldn't. He was quite irritated by her presence but tried not to show it. Lavani was no less annoyed by the presence of people. She sat in a corner, staring at her nails.

Raj was vexed by Lavani's return. He had, before she got married, treated the affair as an investment; he was aware of her father's enormous wealth and his own business needed a miraculous boost; a wealthy sponsor was his most pressing and urgent need. He had met Lavani on a dim evening during a heavy downpour in Bombay. The streets had begun to flood, and she was stranded, holding expensive purchases, with no taxi in sight. He had offered her a lift, which she had readily accepted. Then, the cup of coffee in her expensive home, and the exchange of pleasantries and phone numbers followed. It was she who had fallen in love. He had resisted – not because he was a man of integrity, but because his business was in a lean state and needed attention Then Rajesh, his friend and whiskey partner told him to use the hen who could lay a golden egg, to his advantage. Raj saw sense in what his friend said; he rented an expensive flat for amorous moments with Lavani. He also had to borrow his friend's car, for his own was a small one, and in bad shape.

Lavani had begun her love-life early; had changed many lovers, but Raj was like no other; he seemed to be the final end to her constant search for a satisfying lover. Raj, plagued with business concerns, often played truant on her, which only roused her suspicion and whetted her appetite. She soon started pressing for marriage. Raj, who had initially hidden the fact that he was married, now began to tell her stories – how his wife was demanding two crores as alimony, but he had nothing to give her as his friend had deceived him in business.

After meeting Raj, Lavani began to pester her father for a big investment in Raj's business and clamoured to marry him. Mr. Kumar had already set his detectives on Raj and had found him to be totally unfit to be his son-in-law. Tired of his daughter's dalliances he made up his mind to curb her through marriage. He could not even dream of choosing a groom from Bombay, where Lavani had earned a reputation for being insatiable. It had to be a man from a far off place, where she would not be able to access her ever-ready lovers, and where her reputation would not mar her marriage.

With great sadness, Mr. Kumar told his wife, "In English they diagnose it as nymphomania." It made him feel better to think of his daughter's insatiable appetite as a medical problem. His wife had developed severe asthma after Lavani's third abortion, and his own blood-pressure and diabetes often touched alarming highs. Lavani was their ONLY child. The Kumars were tremendously relieved when the Chandras agreed to accept Lavani as their daughter-in-law. Not only were they financially at par with them, they lived far from Bombay, far enough to remain unaware of Lavani's past.

Lavani put up a stiff resistance to the idea of marriage, but Mr. Kumar was unrelenting. He threatened to disinherit, even disown her. The defiant Lavani was certain that Raj was too much in love with her to let her marry anybody else. She was shocked and hurt when he actually encouraged her to marry the "Mirzapur fellow." He convinced her with the logic that marriage would give her greater freedom to be with him. The truth was that Raj needed to be rid of her. He had not expected such heavy demands on his time and energy as Lavani made.

Instead of money flowing in through her, money was gushing out at incredible speed. Apart from the rent for the flat, he had to pay rent on the furniture that he had hired, and the fridge and the air conditioner....the list was endless.... And the expensive drinks he had to stock for her....the expensive snacks she ate...

Apart from money, another commodity that was fast running out, which he could neither borrow nor hire, was the English Language. Raj had been educated in a vernacular medium school and had acquired only as much of the language as would see him through short-term flirtations with high class women. In his affair with Lavani, which had gone on for seven months, he had to make up for his inadequate English through higher levels of performance on the Kama Sutra front. Lavani spoke only in English, that too with a convent school accent. He had to suppress his pride each time she checked his pronunciation – which was several times a day, and he had now reached bursting point.

"It's not pronounced as you would pronounce 'eight'," she had checked him.

He would fume before his friends: "Now who in saala India pronounces 'ate' as 'et'? She's a masterni, yaar, and I am sick of her." The friends would try to calm him down, reminding him of the crores he could wheedle out of Lavani in case her father died, which could be any day. Raj's cronies had cultivated an acquaintance with a servant from Mr. Kumar's household, who kept them apprised of his escalating blood pressure and cholesterol levels.

It is hard to keep up a smile when you are grimacing mentally, and Raj was on the point of revolt when Lavani told him, much to his relief, that she was under pressure to marry a "bumpkin from a small-town in Uttar Pradesh." That's when Raj began convincing her how marriage would actually give her freedom; how much more fun she could have with him without her father breathing down her neck. And she was finally convinced. She certainly was fed up of her parents nagging her about her affairs. Yes, she could easily dupe that small-town fellow she was marrying. She told Raj that she would soon return after marriage to spend all her life in his lovely flat where they had made love, and only love, and would still do only that in the future. Raj had not believed her when she said that; as soon as she got married he gave up the flat and returned the car. But here she was, back within a few months of her marriage.

Lavani waited impatiently while Raj finalized his deal with the uncouth men who sat in his office. He then took Lavani to a cheap restaurant that was playing loud music; an unkempt waiter dressed in worn out shorts brought water in steel glasses and flung a grubby card on the table. Lavani's face flushed with anger as she walked out of the place. While he followed her out Raj told her he had had a huge loss in business and had to sell the flat and the car and was now living in a friend's house. He would entertain her only if she could salvage him by investing five crores in his business. Lavani walked out of Raj's life, red in the face, her eyes streaming with humiliation and disappointment.

Lavani Moves on, and Further Developments

Lavani had never spent too many days without a lover. She found an even better-looking one this time. Never had anyone loved her as well as John did. Not even Raj.

The Kumars warned Lavani that Robin would divorce her if she stayed away from him. It enraged her to think that "that villager" could have the temerity to divorce her. She was advised by a lawyer to keep spending some time in Mirzapur and keep proof of it, if she wanted to avoid a divorce. So Lavani kept going back to Mirzapur, telling people there that her mother's attacks of asthma had worsened after her marriage and, as the only child, she was compelled to shuttle between her husband and her mother.

Jamal Ansari advised Robin to keep track of all the letters that Lavani wrote and received. Ram Sevak had become adept at intercepting letters, and Robin at re-pasting envelopes. Robin was aghast to see Raj now replaced by a John Fernandes.

Unlike Raj, John was a divorcee. He ran a successful textile business for which he made frequent trips to Varanasi, for raw material. Varanasi which is barely an hour's journey from Mirzapur, is famous for its weaves – its silks, its brocades. John was not merely a wealthy man, he was also a much traveled man who took India's textiles to Europe, America, South East Asia, and the Arab countries.

John's letters to Lavani were less restrained and formal than Raj's, though even he used discretion. But her letters to him surpassed the passion she used to express in her letters to Raj. In her letters to John she liked to paint her husband black and herself a victim: "Waiting for your next trip to Varanasi. What a memorable time we had that night in Hotel Magnifique. You too were magnifique, superb. Ah, what pleasure you gave this unfortunate woman whose husband finds pleasure only in coarse women. Only last evening I caught him with one of the servant girls. Last Sunday he brought home a strange looking young woman who seemed to be a tribal from the neighbouring hills. I have now begun sleeping in the drawing room. I am waiting for someone to end this misery of mine... I live on memories of your love."

Ram Sevak handed Robin a letter from John to Lavani. John had written that he would be visiting Varanasi on the 6th of November and would be staying in Hotel Magnifique. It would give him great pleasure if she could join him for lunch. He would get a chance to discourse on the history of various fabrics in India – a continuation of the discourse during their previous meeting in Hotel Magnifique, he wrote.

The 6th of November was just a week away. According to Jamal Ansari it could be a good opportunity to trap Lavani in the hotel. He even arranged for a private detective. It was not easy to persuade the hotel management to fit cameras and tape recorders in the room that John had booked. Even though the owner of the hotel, Mr. Vaish, was a personal friend of Jamal's cousin, he just wouldn't hear of it, not even after Jamal offered to make a written understanding that the hotel's name would not be used, in case of a court case .Jamal was extremely concerned about Robin's predicament and was at his wit's end as to how to help him. Disappointed in Vaish, he lay awake till the early hours of the morning, thinking of a way out. When he woke up he had a brilliant idea. He thought of approaching his friend, Shyam Singh Chauhan, who was a very senior officer in the Income Tax Department. Shyam was very supportive. He assured Jamal: "There is nothing a businessman fears more than an income tax officer." And sure enough, Mr. Vaish readily agreed to having the detectives plant their cameras and tape-recorders in the hotel room. Jamal reiterated his promise to Mr. Vaish, that the name of the hotel would not be mentioned anywhere, neither in the courts, nor in society.

Jamal observed Robin's sadness and discomfiture at the prospect of having his wife trapped and photographed by strangers. He asked Robin to keep out of the matter until he was required.

Lavani was all excited about the 6 th of November. She told Sumitra that her friend, Pretty Singh, was coming down from Bombay to Varanasi to shop for her wedding and needed her assistance. It would take two days at least to shop around and she and her friend would be staying in the Marwari dharamshala.

The tape recorders taped everything. The cameras photographed everything. On the 6th itself, when Lavani and John went out to have lunch at a Chinese restaurant, the detectives, dressed as hotel staff, saw the photos and heard the tapes. There was enough proof of adultery for a divorce. When Lavani and John returned to the hotel she was taken aside by Jamal and shown some of the evidence. Lavani was quite terrified. Jamal had the divorce papers ready, which she signed without a murmur. She returned directly to Bombay without going to Mirzapur to bid goodbye to her husband or her parents-in-law.

Robin had not imagined that Lavani could be got rid of so smoothly. Jamal had told him of cases in which the divorce proceedings had gone on for as long as thirty years and sometimes a marriage was finally annulled only through the death of one of the spouses.

The Kumars were quite shattered by the prolonged stress that they had been through because of Lavani. Mr. Kumar wound up his business and decided to migrate to Canada where his elder brother ran a chain of restaurants. There existed a close bond between the two and his brother was anxious about Mr. Kumar's failing health; he had repeatedly asked Mr. Kumar to come and stay with him and join him in his business.

Lavani stayed on in India.

Kripa Shankar Nana

Kripa Shankar Pandu, sixty, short, squat, and shabby, was often mistaken for the milkman. The milkman was, however, smarter, and did not go around with a deadpan expression, as KSP did. KSP's family insisted that the shabby clothes and the dull expression were deliberate, and that he was a fraud and a dramebaaz.

The deadpan look disguised a history of daring, and adventure. He had fallen in love at a time when falling in love was taboo in India; he had even "abducted" his bride-to- be. No one could guess from his milkman looks that he was the proprietor of a successful agricultural goods company, that in his youth he had won a scholarship to study engineering in Germany. The Germans had asked him to stay on, had offered him a job, but he was bored stiff in Europe. He missed the chaos and the noise of India, of especially his hometown, Allahabad. Europe was too noiseless, too well- organized, he complained. It was his physicist father who had pushed him into advanced studies. His heart truly lay in rural activities, especially in sorting out the villagers' land disputes with a gun.

Back home, he embarrassed his father who prided himself on his " scientific temper," by enrolling under a spiritual guru who lived in the jungles of Chitrakoot. KSP said he needed to flush out Europe from his being and that he desperately needed a "mental bath." The guru made him chop wood and carry water; he made him cook food for him and tend his cows; he made him gather dung and plaster the floors of his hut with it; he made him press his feet and crack his fingers. KSP slept on the dung-smeared floors, on a bed of straw, in the company of snakes and scorpions. He relished it all, especially cooking on firewood.

The guru tested KSP's nerves with his whimsical changes of mind. But when he was fully convinced of KSP's commitment to spirituality –for which he had tested him enough – the guru opened the secrets of the supernatural to him. He shared powerful mantras and taught him spiritual exercises that would give him the powers of divination.

Eleven months later the guru abruptly asked him to leave.KSP begged to stay on but the guru asked him to go out and be useful. As parting advice, he asked KSP to build a house in which he could keep his brothers with him.

Back home, KSP set up a small factory on the outskirts of Allahabad, manufacturing agricultural machines. His products were a great success and he soon bought the bungalow adjoining his own and constructed three sets of houses around a common courtyard for his two brothers, and himself. He later understood the reason why his spiritual master had asked him to stay close to his brothers. His wife died when he was merely forty-five and he had to bring up his four feisty daughters with the help of his brothers' families and his mother – Amma.

Amma was old and was unable to walk. Her bed occupied a corner of the verandah that overlooked the courtyard, from where she kept an eye on the goings on in the household. Her legs did not support her body, but mentally she was as fit as an acrobat. She was the spice of the earth; no one passed her by without stopping to talk to her – the dhobi, the milkman, the gardener, all liked to stop by her and replenish her knowledge of the neighbourhood, in return for tales from her past. She emerged through those tales as one who could teach the famous feminists a lesson or two in boldness; especially that tale in which she had singlehandedly subdued a dreaded dacoit who was carrying away her mother's jewelry. He and his accomplice were tying up the loot when she came in from behind and threw chilly powder which caused them to cough and cry, almost blinded with tears. In the meantime, she threw kitchen knives at them, hurting them sharply. While they tended to their injuries she raised a cry and the dacoits were overpowered.

When KSP's deadpan look took over we cannot say, but we do know is that in his youth he had fallen in love. The girl's parents raised objections against him based on class and colour; their daughter was fair and pretty, and they themselves were well-placed. They would not accept this swarthy man, who read palms and horoscopes, as their son-in-law. Amma was then physically fit. She garnered a force of milkmen and sweepers and KSP's astrological beneficiaries, and took the girl away. The girl's parents could not even call the police because the Senior Superintendent of Police venerated KSP for of his accurate predictions.

We guess it was when his wife died that the dull look set in.

All day KSP would be in his factory, but by four in the afternoon he would be home, tending his cows, his mother and his children. By evening his verandah would be full of the hopeless and the hopeful, soliciting astrological advice. His guru had probably anticipated his lonely years ahead and had arranged for chaos and cacophony by asking him to house his brothers across the courtyard. The family would connect with each other by hollering across. The house would be perpetually abuzz with carpenters and plumbers and the smell of turpentine would drown the French perfumes the girls dabbed on all day.

It was suspected that Amma was not only a silent accomplice in KSP's outrageous nonconformity, but fully enjoyed it too. If an orthodox Hindu would come visiting, KSP would wear the suit he had got tailored in Saville Row; if he were to have a meeting with a rich and westernized person, he would wear a special pair of worn out rubber chappals and a baniyan that had gone yellow with use.

The din and joire de vive in KPS's home was redoubled when his nephew, Vikram, came to live in it. Vikram was the son of KSP's younger brother who was an architect, living in Chandigarh. Vikram had enrolled as a medical student in the Allahabad Medical College, and KSP would not hear of sending him to hostel. Vikram was swarthy, like his uncle, and somehow, one only focused on his eyes, which were lively and alert. He had the distinction of making even Pukkan laugh. Pukkan, forty-eight, worked for a bank; no one, not even his wife, had ever seen him laugh. Vikram was always on the lookout for the comic – he loved to ruffle the stiff and shock the sober; he could loosen out the sternest of people.

Vikram easily adapted to the ways of Allahabad; the first thing he did was to form a surveillance squad. For the uninitiated, it was natural for every male youngster in Allahabad to "take charge" of his neighbourhood. This kind of initiative accounts for the outstanding number of prime ministers this city has produced. Seven of the prime ministers of India have hailed from Allahabad. Even the most dedicated of students turned "surveyors" by evening, endearing themselves especially to old and sad women. In medieval England such men were known as knights. In more recent times, ever since employment became difficult, boys slog it instead in "coaching institutes," which accounts for the sharp decline in prime ministerial candidates from Allahabad.

A special bond struck up between Vikram and the Joshis. With Batliwala gone the Joshis were rather lonesome and dejected. Vikram often went over to check Joshi's blood pressure. Mrs. Joshi looked forward to his banter. The Joshis liked it when he sometimes stayed overnight to read, in case KSP's home became too noisy. Vikram soon stepped into Raghav's shoes, supervising the electrician and ticking off the gardener. Their own son, the professor of Mathematics in the USA, came for short trips, during which he took his family for sightseeing in India.

Joey Out of College. Comes to live with the Joshis

Joey was now out of school and had entered the Allahabad University as an undergraduate. The Joshis had long been looking forward to having Joey stay with them. They persuaded Mahendra to allow her to stay with them rather than in a hostel. The storm that arose after the Shahnaaz-Raghav wedding had deserted Batliwala's home. Batliwala had left for Australia, soon after, where he died within a year. His wife lingered on for a couple of years, and she too succumbed to heart trouble.

When Batliwala was leaving India he gave the keys to his home to Joshi and had the house willed to Shahnaaz – for Shahnaaz was alive then. After Shahnaaz the house was now registered in Joey's name. The professor never had the heart to enter it; it was Gita, his wife, who had the house dusted and the carpets sunned, from time to time. It was Gita, again, who took Joey into the house, and opened room after room. Stillness lay upon everything – the furniture, the books, the taps. Pictures of the family stood upon the mantelpiece. Gita switched on the lights and turned on the taps. But still the place seemed cold and lifeless.

Joey and Vikram

Much to their disappointment, no friendship grew between Joey and Vikram; Mrs. Joshi shared her puzzlement with an equally puzzled Joshi, "….Our Vikram who is so jovial becomes rather serious in Joey's presence."

"He may be shy of her," said the professor.

"Vikram and shy!!!,"said Mrs. Joshi.

"Well, he doesn't seem the envious sorts, I don't think he would resent her presence here," said the professor.

Mahendra Dies

Following the dramatic turn of events at Hotel Magnifique Robin now applied for a divorce. Soon he would be a free man. But Mahendra never could forgive himself for the grief he had brought upon his most devoted child. He died in sleep even before the divorce was over.

Robin hauled himself out of grief; the friends and relatives had arrived and many would stay on till the last day of mourning – the thirteenth day, which would round off with a feast for all the friends, relatives and acquaintances.

The first thing that Sumitra did, after Mahendra's death, was to remove all the photos of Mahendra's relatives from the mantelpiece in the living room. This sent a clear signal to all his relatives that they would not be welcome in her home any more.

Joey, who had begun counting on Mahendra as her most dependable well-wisher, now felt the full impact of his absence. Robin had been considerably withdrawn from her once she had grown up, and after his marital mishap he withdrew even more. Joey felt lost and out of place in Mahendra's absence. But what made her feel most like an outsider was the deep chasm between Robin and herself. Everyone else comforted Robin for the loss of his father, not she.

Robin kept going into the bathroom to cry out his grief. His eyes would be swollen and red. All the relatives could fling their arms around him, not she. Even when he was suffering Lavani's cruelty and had taken to drinking heavily, she had remained a mute spectator. But there was no one with whom she could share this particular feeling; she could grieve openly for her uncle – it was an acceptable sorrow. But there was no precedent, no legitimacy for a girl grieving over the loss of love in a cousin...perhaps because there would be few precedents for a young man who would mean the world to his little cousin. There was no sanction for the kind of love she had for Robin – neither in mythology nor in the scriptures. He was the most adorable man she had ever known. When amongst others, he held the presence of the insouciant bassist who steals the thunder away from the main performer.... she realized that she adored him at all times, even when he was angry and hateful, even when he was sad and drunk and had spilt food all over his clothes and spoke with that drunken drawl, or walked with that tired drag.

She was determined to love him, especially after Lavani cheated on him and turned everyone, even his parents, against him. She would love him even if raw, pink, cholesterol patches grew above his eyes as had happened with Nimmy Aunty.

Joey knew that no one, not even Robin would understand her feelings for him; orphans are a species apart – they have their own feelings, and their own reasons for holding on to them.

Mahendra's Death and Thereafter

The thirteen days mourning period was interminably long for the family members. One could not switch on the television, one did not eat rich food, play cards or even crack jokes. Cuckoo was bored stiff, and so were his sisters and his wife. Even Sumitra could not sustain such a prolonged mourning.

On the sixth day, Cuckoo, Mohini and Sumitra were sprawled out on Sumitra's king-sized bed. They had shut the door and Cuckoo was hastily consuming salted cashew nuts. Paring her nails, Mohini casually commented on Joey's growing intimacy with Gaumukhi.

"I feel exactly the same as you do," said Sumitra."

"Gaumukhi is sure to tell Joey about her farms and bungalows, now that Papa has gone," said Cuckoo.

"We'll have to do something to keep Joey away from Mirzapur...she's now nineteen and is pretty intelligent for her age," said Sumitra.

"We shall tackle her...let the thirteenth day be over,"said Mohini decisively.

It was the twelfth day of mourning. Joey wanted to light a candle on White Sahib's grave. Gaumukhi went along with her. Karim insisted on accompanying them. On the fifteenth day, when all the guests had left,and Joey too would be returning the following day, Sumitra and Mohini called for Gaumukhi. In Joey's presence they took her to task for encouraging and improper friendship between Joey and Karim. Both Joey and Gaumukhi were speechless with disbelief. Their mouths went dry as Sumitra went on to say to Gaumukhi, "Don't you know that she is an orphan and her izzat is in our chief concern? Evening after evening she sits with that boy, listening to his silly stories. He's only a servant, do you understand?"

When Joey tried to speak Mohini cut her short, saying, "You are not coming to Mirzapur until you get over this boy. OK, Miss?"

Sumitra also had the matter conveyed to Robin. Robin, whose nerves were already jangled, looked into Joey's eyes and said, "In our family women do not visit the servants' quarters." He spelt out each word clearly. Joey stood stunned. Gaumukhi took her aside and asked her to leave at once. She reminded herself that she was the same unfortunate woman who had once asked Shahnaaz and Raghav to leave the Mirzapur home.

Gaumukhi asked Robin to arrange for Joey's journey.

This is how Joey's cord with Mirzapur snapped. And also her cord with Robin.

Gaumukhi wanted to leave the Bungalow but was too wise to leave it right away. She was also too wise to tell Karim all that had happened. She told him instead that Sumitra had accused her of inciting Joey against the family. Karim was enraged, but Gaumukhi cautioned him against making a scene, for Joey's sake. They decided they would leave Mirzapur and seek employment in Allahabad, so as to be close to Joey, but at an opportune moment, be it a month or two later, so that Joey would not be linked with their leaving.

Joey Returns to Allahabad Sad

This was Joey's saddest journey, at par with the journey to Mirzapur from Africa, when her parents died. Only then she was not as lonely as she felt today. The person she had loved and trusted had set his back upon her; the estrangement with Robin was unbearable.

As the car moved towards Allahabad bitter thoughts raced through her mind....The love that Robin had once showered upon her was not for her sake, thought she...he had done it for his father; he had taken care of his father's niece; he had never loved her....never had he proclaimed in public that she was his sister. And why would he care for her...she was just an orphan....Ever since she had grown up he had distanced himself from her, as if she were a pariah....When his marriage broke he would stay away from home, or would be drinking hard, even when she was around...never did he allow her to comfort him...How she had longed to hold him and tell him that she would always be there for him....When Mahendra died he was beside himself with grief, she could only stand and stare, while that divorcee cousin of his, who came down from Paris, threw her arms around him and they stayed up all night – several nights. Bitter thoughts raced through her head; life was not worth living anymore....no one loved her.... even the Joshis cared for her out of a sense of duty...they were more fond of that joker – Vikram – that Vikram who played the fool with every milkmaid on the streets but had never a word to say to her – ONLY because she was an ORPHAN.

Mohini Enters Mirzapur

Mohini began to visit Mirzapur more often after Mahendra's departure, under the pretext of comforting Sumitra. Her visits enabled her to keep track of the farm produce, in which Cuckoo had an equal share; he was also entitled to rent from the five houses that the family had let out. To say nothing of the buried treasure. Mohini was not one to trust anyone.

Robin had never liked Mohini; much but now he welcomed her; with Mahendra gone there was no one with whom he could discuss the problems of the factory and the farms. The establishment was always a complex one to handle, and now there was the additional responsibility of the garden and the orchards. Mahendra had run the garden to perfection; Robin was losing his sleep over leaf-curl and aphids. Mohini was the woman with practical solutions to problems, she could deal with them without getting agitated. As for Sumitra, she trusted Mohini more than she trusted her own offspring. She would wait to confide her fears and suspicions in her.

On her second visit to Mirzapur, Mohini suggested that some of the burden on Robin's head be eased. For example, the bungalow near the river be sold off, as also the farm on the west side. Sumitra understood and agreed, though hesitantly. The bungalow belonged to Raghav and Robin was planning to run a hotel in it. Mohini, venal as she was, resented that Robin should get the benefit of Raghav's properties. But if sold, Cuckoo would get a share of the proceeds. Mohini said she feared Joey might get to know about these properties and sell them off to the wrong people.

Robin had set his heart on the bungalow, and he was getting handsome returns from Raghav's farm. So he came to an understanding with his brother: he would get the bungalow registered in Cuckoo's name by bribing the authorities after showing Raghav-Shahnaaz's death certificate; he would then purchase the bungalow off him. He would do something similar with the farm. This way Cuckoo and Mohini would be assuaged of their fears that

Robin was enjoying the lion's share of the assets in Mirzapur.

Some matters cannot be hidden; both Ram Sevak and Karim came to know of the buying and selling going on. Both Ram Sevak and Gaumukhi knew that both the properties belonged to Joey. Ram Sevak tendered his resignation in disgust and went back to his village to tend to the small patch of land he possessed. Karim rushed to Allahabad to apprise the Joshis and Joey of the impending sale. Joey had no attachment to property but it broke her heart to be cheated upon by Robin. She refused to assert her right to the property, happy to give it to Robin for having loved her in her childhood. Karim was disappointed in her attitude.

Robin's deceitfulness wiped out the little faith that Joey had in him. And she began to sink into deep depression, not sleeping nights. Not a morsel of food would go down her throat. She would choke even on water.

The Joshis were concerned and consulted Vikram about it. Vikram had been too busy with exams to visit the Joshis. He rushed to Joey when he came to know about her. Joey was sitting in the veranda on the steps that lead into the garden. Her anguish was writ upon her face. It wrenched his heart to see her. He sat on the steps, saying nothing. Joey walked away.

Karim and Gaumukhi move to Allahabad

Already vexed with the accusations hurled at them after Mahendra's death, Karim and Gaumukhi were no longer happy to be at the Bungalow. They decided to move to Allahabad; Gaumukhi missed Joey very much. So one fine morning Karim and Gaumukhi landed at Joshis, bag and baggage and asked if they could stay with them till they got a room on rent. "Why, there's a big house here for you to stay and look after," said the Professor, referring to Batliwala's house.

Joey was overjoyed to see Karim and Gaumukhi. Gaumukhi began to help Mrs. Joshi, and Karim contemplated setting up a garage nearby. Their bickerings brightened up the Joshis' household. Vikram took to Karim instantly, and so did KSP. KSP would not hear of Karim opening a garage; he appointed him supervisor in his factory.

The three orphans: Gaumukhi, Karim, and Joey were together again. Joey began to heal. Karim kept in touch with the Bungalow through the servants who kept him informed about the developments there. Robin was going through utter dejection and had taken to drinking heavily. He missed his old faithful servants and persuaded Ram Sevak to return to the Bungalow.

Robin was preparing to go on a business trip to the United States when a neighbour, Mr. Patti called on him. Mr. Patti was a simple, honest sort of a man, but very successful in his carpet business. He had begun advising Robin in matters of business. Robin had developed a high trust in him. One day Mr. Patti called on Robin in a broken state; he had recently come to know that his daughter, whom he had married off a few months ago to a doctor in New York, had discovered that her husband was already married to an American woman and had a child with her. The doctor had married his daughter under parental pressure and had kept his earlier marriage a secret; the son of a business tycoon, he feared his father would disinherit him if he came to know about the American wife. Confronted with the truth by his Indian wife he turned her out of the house and she was now staying with a distant relative in America. Mr. Patti told Robin his grief and requested him to arrange to bring back his daughter, Anuradha, to India. On reaching America, Robin met Anuradha. Anuradha was a simple, quiet sort of a girl. Her distress moved Robin.

An instant attraction grew between Robin and Anuradha, ending in marriage. The wedding was a quiet affair and Joey was invited. Joey took Karim and Gaumukhi along for the wedding. Suffering often contracts the heart, joy often opens it. Robin was so happy with his lovely wife that he began to return to his old, affectionate self. He asked Joey to sell her farms and the riverfront bungalow to him, which she did.

Shashank Kapoor

During her depression Joey had not been attending classes. One evening a young professor, one of Joey's teachers, Shashank Kapoor, paid her a visit. From his looks and demeanour he seemed a gentle and cultured sort. He sat and chatted with the Joshis who were floored by his pleasant manners and good looks. He soon became a regular visitor.

Though he chatted with the Joshis it was clear that he came to meet Joey. He discussed the topics that Joey had missed and even brought her some reading material. Joey was touched and promised Shashank that she would resume attending her classes. The Joshis who were concerned about Joey's depression began to feel grateful to Shashank for his concern for Joey. They encouraged him to come more often. Shashank took up this request and began visiting Joey more often. He was interested in Joey, though not in love with her. His parents were pressurizing him for marriage and Joey was one of the girls he had found suitable for an arranged marriage.

Joey was a bit nonplussed about Shashank's visits but she thought he was making them to meet Joshi Nana who was his colleague in the University. It was not the right protocol in those days for a teacher to visit his student on a social level. Marriage was almost taboo. Joey thus looked upon Shashank as Joshi Nana's visitor whom she had to entertain, being his student. In those days a teacher was much revered and the distance between the teacher and the taught was a considerable one. The Joshis too were initially confused about Shashank's visits. Shashank did not hide the fact that his visits were for Joey alone. The Joshis began to draw hope from the fact that Shashank could be a potential suitor for Joey. He looked the caring and gentle sorts, which would be the best thing for Joey.

The Joshis began to weave dreams of love for Joey; the young man was from a good family, he was pleasant and, what was more, he liked our Joey. They shared these happy possibilities with Vikram.

"The best part of all this is that he is such a gentle person," a visibly excited Mrs. Joshi gurgled before Vikram. All the brightness vanished from Vikram's face. He fell silent.

"What is your opinion on this matter?"pursued Mrs. Joshi. The Joshis were taken aback by Vikram's response. He got up and walked away.

Vikram was back within half an hour. He lashed out at the Joshis:

"You allow all sorts of people to come into the house. And you like them for liking her. I thought it was the unwritten rule in Allahabad – at least in my gang – that you don't fall in love with your host's daughter, or ward."

"What is wrong with falling in love?, "asked a perplexed Prof. Joshi.

"Nothing wrong with that," retorted Vikram. "No decent teacher will ever visit his student the way this fellow does. What are his intentions in coming here? Were I in your place I would kick him out."

The Joshis were very confused. Vikram was not entirely wrong in what he had said. But the Joshis wanted Joey to settle down, and they liked Shashank.

"Looks like Vikram has brotherly feelings towards Joey....I too used to be very possessive about my sisters," said the professor to his wife.

"If he has brotherly feelings then let him approach Shashank about Joey," said Gita.

So the next time Vikram visited them the professor brought up the matter with him. Vikram went livid in the face and refused to carry the matter any further. On his way back, Vikram found Joey standing at the gate.

"Waiting for Shashank, aren't you," said Vikram.

"What do you mean," she said.

"Shashank Kapoor is handsome so he stands a good chance with girls," said Vikram, feeling very stupid having uttered those words. Joey was both perplexed and annoyed by Vikram's words.

"You can't speak to me like that, he is my teacher," said Joey.

"He is your teacher, and I am only your doctor. When you get high fever I sit up all night by your bedside......but he is your teacher and he is handsome."

Saying this, Vikram walked out. Joey stood perplexed. It was true that Vikram spent much time by her bedside whenever she was sick. But he spoke so little to her that she thought he was obliging the Joshis.

It was a clear September sky. Joey sat at the window watching white clouds race by, Vikram's words "...and I am only your doctor....but he is your teacher and he is handsome" kept going through her mind. There was something comforting in his anger; her woman's instinct made her feel calm within.

Vikram did not turn up three days and Joey was impatient to meet him. She sat on the garden steps, waiting for him. Suddenly KSP Nana turned up wearing his worst clothes, clutching a bowl in hand. He put the bowl at Joshi's feet, begging for Joey's hand for Vikram.

The Joshis, confused by this sudden happening, asked Joey point blank. Karim who was witness to this scene yelled with glee and thanked Allah, for according to him, Vikram was the best choice for Joey.

"Say yes," he coaxed Joey.

Joey hugged KPS Nana and set aside his bowl. The Joshis began to cry. It was not their tears alone that they shed but Raghav and Shahnaaz's as well. And the Batliwalas'. Vikram was soon at Joshi's place, tears streaming down his cheeks when Joshi handed Joey's hand to him.

Vikram had to make a lot of explanations to Joey: why he did not speak openly to her earlier; how it was love at first sight for him. Gradually he was able to convince her.

A heavy weight went off the Joshis' hearts. Their beloved Vikram would marry an equally beloved Joey.

Robin and Joey Re-Unite. Vikram and Joey Marry

Happiness washes off bitterness. So it happened with Robin who was now happily married. He decided to return to Joey all that was hers. He even announced that Joey's wedding would take place in Mirzapur and he would give the bride away.

What more happiness could Joey want than to be given away by the person she loved the most! This was the tale of two cities, united by a river and united by love. A tale of love and yearning, of knots tying up and opening. Who would have thought the tale would have so many bends. Joey had completed Raghav's story.

ᗡᗡᗡ

Tolas are places associated with particular people. Till the early nineties there were several Bengali tolas in Allahabad. Mumfordgunj, where I lived as a child, was not exactly a Bengali tola but four of the houses next to ours belonged to Bengalis.

Ours was the only house of a non-Bengali on the street. Four houses away from ours stood Bapi da's house, next to Oindrilla's. Oindrilla was my classmate; we went to school in the same bus. Five other girls our age-group caught the bus at Oindrilla's gate. Waiting for the bus, we would peep into Bapi da's garden which was the best that I had ever seen. We often strayed in, to finger the pink roses or to gush over the dog flowers or the nasturtiums. My favourite was the pale blue morning glory on the bower.

In the evening we would assemble at Oindrilla's house (which shared a fence with Bapi da's) to play. The ball would often go over the indrabela fence and I was usually sent to fetch it. I would linger in the garden to look at the flowers, pretending, of course, to be looking for the ball.

Bapi da's mother would sit in the veranda, reading. The black Labrador would lie at her feet. She was a good friend of my mother and I called her Mashima, or aunt. I grew up admiring the heavy Edwardian furniture in her home; also her gold bangles and her saris. Their home had a wholesome air about it, supported by the smells of gourmet cooking.

Bapi was the scholarly types, a book addict, and preferred solitude. But he was attached to our family, being my brother's (Anand da's) friend. Anand da was six years my senior; I had been a late child so my parents hardly supervised my upbringing. They just let me be. My school reports were atrocious, especially the Mathematics part. Anand da took over the parenting role, becoming my virtual father. Such a watchful brother he made, and what an impatient Mathematics teacher! He also taught me how to sit in a ladylike manner – not with my legs apart. He would check my bags for comics and romances. I was to read Charles Dickens and other classics, instead.

When I turned thirteen, Anand da won a scholarship for further studies in Cambridge and when he went I lived onwards almost like an only child.

After Anand da left, Bapi da would make short but frequent visits to our place, checking out on our welfare. It was on one of these visits that mother told Bapi da about my difficult relationship with Mathematics and the sciences. Bapi da assured her he would look into my difficulties. And he did, successfully. I could not help boasting that Bapi da had helped me with Mathematics and my image went up immediately amongst my friends. I was treated with a respect I had not tasted before. During cricket I was now allowed to bat, whereas I had always been only a fielder. Bapi da was universally respected.

We were now into our teens and the playful days were soon over. We sat on Oindrilla's terrace late into the evening sharing juicy personal things. We shared bra-talk, period problems and our current heart-throbs.

Time passed. We entered university, but Oindrilla's terrace remained the hub of our meetings. Oindrilla was not a bad student but she was not interested in studies. Though we went to the same university and had offered similar subjects, our choice of friends had changed. I had few friends, Oindrilla had several. She was charming and vivacious and naturally attracted friends. She exuded the confidence that offspring of wealthy parents often do. My parents were not wealthy. We were just comfortable. And even if my father had been a wealthy man his temperament was such that he would keep us deprived. Ever since he had touched Gandhiji's feet he had taken up the vow of asceticism. I grew up a timid girl, afraid of people, especially men. God compensated me by giving me an intense love for Nature, and I spent more time with plants than with human beings.

I admired Bengali women for the way they dressed up. The perfumes I had inhaled during Durga Puja gatherings are still fresh in my memory. How lovely the Bengali women looked in the Puja pandals! In the pandals the boys would chase the girls and there would be much laughter and banter. No boy ever teased me; I dressed plainly and was the serious sorts. I envied my friends whose boyfriends joked and flirted with them. I longed for a boyfriend. And on Holi day I would shut myself in the bathroom and apply red colour to the parting of my hair to see in the mirror how I would look as a bride.

Oindrilla had many admirers who went up and down the street to get a glimpse of her. Despite the difference in our personalities she still befriended me, for she needed someone she could trust with her secrets, her loves and her longings. Some of her boyfriends were non-Bengalis; the one she admired most was Praveen who came from a wealthy business family. I doubted whether her parents would allow her to marry him. Praveen was a flashy fellow and I am sure the Bengalis preferred sober sons-in-law. When I warned her against him, she made fun of me and said that those who fear never get anywhere in life. I do not know whether she meant that for me but I still did admire her for her oomph and her chutzpah.

Oindrilla continued to confide in me. Praveen had kissed her and she was on cloud nine. She began to meet Praveen more regularly on the sly.

One day Oindrilla sent for me through her gardener. I thought she might be unwell and rushed to her. Oindrilla shut the door and whispered, "Arre that sneak of a Devyani Mukerjee tattled against me and Praveen to Ma. I am not allowed to go to the University anymore. Am not allowed to even go near the phone." I felt extremely concerned for Oindrilla but there was not much I could do. I was sent for again after a week. I adjusted my mind to a sympathetic frame, ready to commiserate with Oindrilla over her forced separation from Praveen. How cruel parents can be, I thought. I anticipated meeting a swollen eyed Oindrilla but to my surprise I found her looking radiant and happy.

"Guess what, Meetu, I am engaged!."

"Oh, so they have relented towards Praveen,"said I, feeling very glad for her.

"Thut! Not Praveen. Guess who?"

"I can't," said I.

"It's Bapi, "she said, hugging me.

"Bapi da!"

"Yes Bapi. Oh Meetu, I'm so happy. Bapi is so rich, I will not have to work either in the house or outside."

The turn of events was most unexpected. Nevertheless I put on a show of happiness. Oindrilla made a gorgeous bride. Bapi da made a happy but sober bridegroom.

When I visited Oindrilla next, in Bapi da's home, I was surprised to see the change in her. She was dressed as a traditional Bengali married woman with vermilion in the parting of her hair and the red and white paula and shankha bangles. She played the perfect daughter-in-law, touching her in- laws' feet and participating in the puja, morning and evening. Mashima was obviously pleased with her and Bapi da looked content. He even joked with me a little, unlike the serious Bapi da I knew. Oindrilla had brought life into the Chakravartis' home. The Labrador followed her wherever she went and Oindrilla sang for Mashima and even cooked fish.

Time rolled on. In the meantime, I got a job in the University of Allahabad, where I had studied. But life continued to be tough. My father died of Hodgkin's disease and my mother had a brain stroke soon after. My brother had settled down in England and could come to India only once a year. I was getting lonely. With my father gone, my prospects of marriage looked bleak. Sometimes I missed Bapi da's visits to check us out. Now as a lawyer he was busy. Besides, he was married. Two years had passed since Oindrilla's marriage. Both of us were busy in our own worlds and met only fleetingly. One day she sent for me, to meet her at her parents' home where she was for a brief stay. It was urgent, her maid said. I was, as always, concerned, and rushed to meet her. Oindrilla bolted the door from inside.

"Look Meetu, you have known me all along. You know I am not the sort of person to be happy with someone like Bapi. He is a good man, no doubt, but I am bored stiff.

He works till late, preparing court cases. After that do you think he has any energy left for me?”

“But what is the solution?” I asked, dazed.

“Oindrilla has a solution for every problem, she said. “You remember Praveen? Well, I have been in touch with him. He is still interested in me and wishes to take me away to Dubai where he has a very good job.”

Bapi da and Mashima swum before my eyes. They would be broken.

“You can’t do that to Bapi da,” I protested.

“Well, I am not to blame. My mother cajoled me into this marriage to keep me away from Praveen who was not a Bengali. Anyway, I have asked Bapi for a divorce and he has agreed. I told him about Praveen. Bapi will get us married in a temple.

My head began to swim. “What was Bapi da’s reaction when you told him about Praveen?”

“He had caught us meeting on the sly. It was he who proposed the divorce and the wedding instead of us meeting on the sly.”

“Oh how magnanimous Bapi da is, ”I couldn’t help saying.

“I don’t know,” she replied. “He confessed that he wasn’t happy with this marriage either. He had married me to please his mother; on his own he would have married somebody less of an extrovert.”

“Am I shallow?”asked Oindrilla. I didn’t know what to say.

The divorce came through. Oindrilla was married off in a temple in the presence of neighbours and friends. This way Bapi da would not have to explain the future absence of his wife.

Mashima was initially upset but she soon saw wisdom in her son's decision. Life began returning to normal and Bapi da resumed his trips to our home to check on us. Both mother and I had now something to look forward to. We always brightened up at the sight of him, especially since he had started shouldering the difficult tasks like payment of taxes and handling the domestic-help who had started taking advantage of our helplessness. Somewhere within me was this deep conviction that Bapi da would always be there for us. Life was so much happier with him around.

4
The Clock

It had to be...I had to smash that Clock some day. Had it been one of those silent types that simply told the time I would have let it be, but this one sang it in joyous, extended notes. In any case it was out of place in the staff-room where nothing ever seemed to change.

The smashing made all the difference – or so I imagined then. I was soon to realize that the real clock lay within the mind and that mine was stuck at some moment of anger. To come back to the smashing, as I said, it had to be done some day. It may not have changed things in the long run, but as the paper-weight hit the clock a heavy silence fell upon the staff-room. All the buggers in there dropped their coffee-house bonhomie and fell silent. They sat hushed as I walked out into what I felt was a brave new world.

But friend, the smashing of the clock neither makes one brave nor the world new. If the colleagues were shocked when the smash occurred they were rather composed, as if such happenings were a part of adult experience. Subsequently, they exchanged meaningful glances whenever I entered the staff-room.

I had begun to feel rather uneasy, as if I was abnormal.

Two days after the incident, my elder brother paid me a visit. From his uncharacteristic good humour towards me I guessed that he had heard and had come to talk over matters. My brother, an engineer turned successful businessman, has disentangled his nerves with the help of meditation and the blessings of his Swamiji. He is the author of pearls of wisdom like:

"If you cannot bend a ray of light towards yourself you can, at least, open a window."

Brother fixed his gaze towards me, mentally looking for a foothold for his talk. I felt a discourse coming. Soon he would, in his measured Vedantic tones, be talking about the need for introspection, self-integration and the like.

Brother's discourses are devastating in their length. He pins you down totally, not allowing even a shift of gaze; you emerge from them dizzy, and totally disoriented. He was warming himself up with the preamble when I said I had to go to the loo.

I must have sat there a good twenty minutes, doing nothing. Through the window I could see the skies; they were a winter blue, with much traffic through them. The parrots were in a desperate hurry to reach somewhere. They screeched anxious messages on the way; the pigeons swiftly flew across; but they were not in a hurry, it was just their speed. The eagles hovered leisurely. No hurry to get anywhere.

The door banged. I saw brother through the window, walking energetically towards the gate.

I was by now feeling quite uncomfortable about the whole affair and in my mind was often conducted a General Body Meeting of all teachers "to discuss the act of vandalism by a young teacher of the Department of English and Modern European languages."

Pandey rose to the podium:

"As President of the Allahapur University Teachers' Association it is incumbent upon me to voice the general concern and consternation amongst the faculty about the breach of decorum by Dr. Shambhu Sharma of the Department of English...."

Pandey's tone revived with nostalgia the crisp announcements that echoed over the public address system on the Annual Prize day at school:

"Shambhu Sharma of class Nine, Section D, gets the First prize for English, and the first prize for Hindi Elocution."

Thunderous applause.

Everything about Pandey gleamed: his glasses, his watch, his face. He was always travelling to seminars and conferences.

Then Bhattacharya rose to the occasion, his spectacles falling off, his curls all over his forehead:

"Sir, in keeping with the lofty traditions of this glorious university which is now one hundred and thirty years old, we must condemn Mr. Sharma's act of vandalism in the strongest possible terms...."

Bhattacharya could not proceed; he had, as usual, taken the high note too soon. He was trembling all over, choking with emotion. Saxena, who had been dying to speak, quickly usurped the pause:

"We cannot, and we will not, tolerate this kind of indiscipline," he announced with the passion of a patriot. But Bhattacharya had not yet finished; he and Saxena faced each other like curs set for a fight while Agarwal begged our attention.

In the University my friends were few. They stayed away from the meeting. I was surprised when the harmless looking Arora from the Hindi department condemned me in chaste Hindi That after I had helped him reverse his car in the market just the other day. He was having problems doing it.

Also among others who lynched me verbally were "Yellow Teeth," "Wolf in Buddha's Clothing," and "I am Lord of all I Survey." Lord Survey's ire against me was understandable. I had only recently refused to succumb to his niece in marriage. He had invited me over a cup of tea which turned out to be a sumptuous feast during which he materialized his thick-lipped niece who looked as though she was going to burp, but never did. How I wriggled out of that mess is another story.

But how had I ever harmed Yellow Teeth and Wolf in Buddha's Clothing? Lord bless me, my colleagues gave them names, not I.

Pandey resumed the podium after three hours. Thumping the table for attention, he informed the august body that the matter would now be referred to the Vice Chancellor for action.

The VC sent for me. He was very civil, very guarded. He offered me tea and biscuits and discussed the problem of funds and delayed sessions. It made me squirm to be spoken to as an adult; the man to man position was intolerable. I wanted him to bring the matter up though I wondered how I would explain myself in so brief and formal a meeting. But he did not mention the clock at all.

I was wretched. I wanted to shout in the hoarse voice of the hysterical (like the deprived in Marxist Indian films) but my problem was too subtle to be telescoped into shout-worthy accusations. Besides, I was not deprived/oppressed I was simply irritated. Irritated as only a teacher of English in India can be.

My brethren, in this vast confusion called India, English is not just a language – it is the Goal, the Aspiration, the Promised Land. So brethren, he who attaineth the title of a university teacher of English is an envied man, be he ever paid so little. Be it the bowel of any, doctor, engineer or merchant, it churneth with envy for professor of English. And they stop him in the streets, yea even in the market, to ask him meaning of this word and that. They say, "Tell which is older, prehistoric or antediluvian." If the Master of English, busy assessing tomatoes pauseth to think, a gleam of victory doth come to the eye of the questioner that doth proclaim: "This blighter hath become teacher of English!."

And that retired Commissioner of Revenue interrupts his morning walk and mine to recite with emphatic rhythm inspirational lines from the 1860s, only so that he may ask me patronizingly who is the author of those lines, so that all on the street may know the great difference between his generation and mine.

All this I undergo for wages so meagre, my grocer doth pity me.

All you teachers of History, Commerce, Economics, who sit in judgment over me, you do not know what it is to be teacher in the Dept. of English and Allied Hassles. You only teach your subject, you don't have to live it. Nor do you have to watch your colleagues adopting strange postures to adapt to Englishness. You don't have a Gupta in your department who is obliged to be caustic because he teaches Swift, nor a Tandon who strives to be a misfit in honour of Shelley. Then there is Mun Mun who sends chills down your spine with her bombastic vocabulary and her clipped accent. If you pronounce the 't' in debut then don't apply for post of cook at Mun Mun's. But speak faulty Hindi and good English and you can dine with her. Her insides are all gnawed up by feminism and activism and her muscles are all tensed up upholding the best traditions of spoken English.

Then there is Capoor, Mun Mun's equally chilling counterpart in the male species. Capoor keeps the mandatory beard of the avant garde. He walks in English, talks in English, laughs purely in English, coughs in English, shrugs his shoulders in American English, and all this before students who walk in Hindi, smile in Hindi and cannot afford woolens in winter.

If Capoor were all, the Clock would still be fostered by silence and slow time. But he heads a cult and his followers taunt you to shreds if they catch you eating anything Hindi in the bazaar. And there is not one man in the department who'd stand up to them and say: "You sit on your ass, I sit on mine, so what is it to you what I eat and how I live. What is it to you if I fast on Mondays, visit temples on Tuesdays, do the trek to Vaishno Devi, or wear stones for luck?

Brother, thou whose nerves Vedanta hath strengthened, teach me to bear up with all the sorts who make up the world. But thy discourses I do dread. My intestines are so knotted up with the strain of holding up this bridge between Shakuntala and Desdemona, that they are hard like a cricket ball. If you could, in your wisdom not be perturbed when the neighbourhood boys smashed your window instead of the wicket, can you not forgive me if I picked up the paperweight and....

ᐅᐅᐅ

5

Polly

Rajiv's wife, who was a Latvian, had left him recently. He was relieved that she had taken the children along. Over the past two years he had been observing a growing attachment between his daughters, Ria and Sherry, and Bruce Martin. Ria was eight and Sherry six. He later understood that his wife, Tanya, had planted an intimacy between Bruce and the girls to ensure a smooth future when she moved out to live with him.

Bruce was an Australian, tall and energetic, with an easy smile. In fact, you could not imagine him without the smile. The girls would hang round his neck, their feet dangling in the air, and there would be much laughter and squealing when they were with him. Bruce lived next door with a golden retriever the girls loved to play with. Rajiv disliked dogs and firmly dismissed his daughters' plea for one. In one of her bad moods Tanya said she had heard that Indians were too stingy and selfish to keep pets. Rajiv retorted without looking up from the newspaper, "I have heard that Indian girls make excellent wives."

According to Rajiv, until Bruce moved next doors Tanya went around looking like a corpse, constantly whining about this and that and about the weather. Rajiv wondered why he had married her, of all people. He had little patience with low-voiced women who came down with colds and headaches if you took them out on a picnic.

In all his life Rajiv had fallen in love only once, when he was fourteen, in the year 1970. That was right after his family shifted to Allahabad along with his father's regiment. She lived in the adjoining neighourhood. Polly Sengupta, thirteen, was plump and spirited – the cutest girl he had ever seen. Rajiv made frantic trips up and down her street, only to get a glimpse of her. He was certain she knew that he liked her, for she would, very discreetly come out, now gathering flowers for the vases, now pretending to check whether the milkman had shut the gate or not. Her mother kept a garden, which had to be protected from goats and cows that wandered about all over the city. He had sensed that Polly was afraid of her parents.

Rajiv thanked God that Polly had no brother. Her sister, Millie, who was not much older, gave him meaningful smiles, which were very reassuring. Polly's father was big built and no gentle giant; in the neighbourhood he was referred to as "Volcano," Polly's mother was sharp-tongued and inflammable; her pets, the dachshunds, would rush for safe cover under the beds when she was in a temper, which was several times a day.

Every Thursday, Mr. Sengupta would send Polly to the Tankhas' place to fetch a mango sprig. The sprig had to have five leaves, as was required for Lakshmi puja. The Tankhas were an elderly couple who had mango, guava, jackfruit, kinnow, pomegranate and lemon trees in their backyard. Mr. Tankha had a passion for trees, and Mrs. Tankha for animals.

Though Mr. Tankha was in his late sixties, he was a magnet for young people. He read their palms and told each one of them that they would change the world and make it a better place, and that he would watch all this happen from Above. He talked poetry and politics and human values with them and subjected them to Socratic pokes. Many a bored and listless young soul found stimulation in his company. Not wealthy by any means, he was immensely rich.

Rajiv considered it a privilege to be a part of the young company at the Tankhas' place and soon became their blue-eyed boy. He had practical skills beyond his years, he could mend any machine, and, when the need arose, could improvise gadgets on the spot. He had made the Tankhas' life much easier.

Rajiv had never exchanged a word with Polly. It was only on Thursdays that he would get the chance to gauge the flush that rose to her cheeks at the sight of him. Five Thursdays went well for him but the following sixth proved unlucky. It had been a terrible mistake on his part to have handed the Senguptas' milkman first a five rupee note and then a note for Polly. Of course, he hadn't mentioned her name:

My darling,

I did not see you yesterday. I want to tell you that a day that goes without a glimpce of you is a day gone waste. I cannot tell you how much I adore you.

Yours to the last and final breadth.

Your eternal lover,

Rajiv.

These expressions of love went straight into Mr. Sengupta's hands. He strode up to the Colonel's house and hollered out his name from the street. There were no introductions, no preamble, only a plain statement:

"If your son is seen near my house again I will throw him into the Ganga, where crocodiles will chew him up."

Mrs. Sengupta, who was a teacher of English, hung on to the spelling mistakes and interspersed them among other accusations:

"Let your son learn the spellings of simple words like "glimpse" before he writes love letters to properly educated girls from decent families. Control your son, Col. Rai, or I will go to his school and get him rusticated," she threatened, thrusting the love-note into his face.

The Senguptas kicked up such a storm that there was no way out for Col. Rai but to send Rajiv away from Allahabad to his grandparents in Delhi.

They say that when God shuts one door He opens another. In Rajiv's case many more doors flung open and life became more exciting than ever. Nothing could induce him to study. By the age of eighteen he was all intent to cross seas in search of work and independence. The construction company that had employed him in Saudi Arabia found him hardworking and ingenious. It took him along to Croatia, South Africa, Papua New Guinea, and finally, to America.

Rajiv decided to stay on in America where he took up odd jobs and soon worked his way up. The citizenship took quite a while but it was well worth the waiting. It was in America that he had met Tanya in a restaurant. She was dining alone and so was he, and they got talking. She was soft spoken and slender and looked like she might need his help with gadgets. Rajiv was pretty lonesome himself. They were married within a fortnight.

With that hasty marriage, history had repeated itself in Col. Rai's family: like father like son, they all said.

Col. Rai was the oldest of the six offspring of Govardhan Rai, Esq., for that is how his nameplate proclaimed him. Govardhan Rai was a wealthy landowner; the "Esq." was a palliative for not having been knighted by the Queen. His hangers-on kept alive the regret by referring to his "monumental stature" in society. They pleaded knighthood for him on grounds of his "profound" knowledge of English Literature.

Govardhan Rai had got his BA degree from Allahabad University, which was one of the first four universities of India. He could still quote lines from Bacon and Shakespeare. Quotes from Bacon and Milton defined his persona in public, but within a closed, intimate group, his favourite wisdom-saying was: "It is better to have loved and lost than to never have loved at all." His favourite lines in poetry were:

Come into the garden, Maud,
For the black bat, night has flown,
Come into the garden Maud,
I am here at the gate alone;
And the woodbine spices are wafted abroad,
And the musk of the roses blown.

Tennyson may not have intended as much yearning in these lines as the Esquire's rendition evoked among his audience. Tears would spring to their eyes, already moist from whiskey. However, Govardhan Rai kept his romantic strain well under leash. You could not be a romantic and succeed as a landowner; rather you had to display your ease with the gun to keep mango thieves and rivals in check. But blood will not be suppressed, and the romantic gene erupted in his son, the Colonel, and yet again in his grandson, Rajiv – both of whom married on impulse.

Colonel Raghav Rai had, in his youth, stunned everybody by marrying an Anglo Indian girl, Roberta. Roberta liked her whiskey and cigarettes. She wore pants and high skirts. She even rode a scooter in those times when Indian women were neither meant to be seen nor heard. Hell broke loose when Raghav announced his decision to marry her. A loud chorus reached the skies:

"He did not even think of his sisters! Who is going to marry into this family now! All three shall die spinsters."

Goverdhan Rai's wealth came to his rescue. He doubled his daughters' share of dowry and all three of them found good homes where they were treated well, despite the Roberta factor in their family. Raghav Rai could now raise a toast to his feisty wife, but never could he interfere with his sons'choices in life. He had three sons – each of them was willful and stubborn.

Col. Rai fumed silently: this Rajiv fellow had gone too far by marrying this Latvian girl. It would have still made sense had the girl been from England or France. But Latvia! He had to bring out his big and heavy atlas again and again to show his family and friends where Latvia was. As for himself, he had married a girl from his own country and he at least knew which religion she belonged to. He had no answer when the old women in his family demanded to know the Latvian girl's caste.

Raghav was furious about Tanya. His sisters pacified him by bringing up the example of his own wife, Roberta, the turnaround in whose reputation, from social reject to savior, had acquired the status of a parable.

Roberta belonged to Goa. She walked like she owned the earth and laughed as if nothing could ever go wrong. She could fix a fuse better than her brother, who was shy and long-haired and played the piano.

She could even get under the car to fix the tyre. When she fell in love with Raghav Rai there was mourning in both her family and his. Her family lamented the loss of her presence, for she was the one who could deal with any emergency that fell upon them. They feared their hearty Roberta would suffocate to death in the medieval dungeons of Uttar Pradesh where women were stored indoors to rot in a stew of male domination and feminine intrigue.

But fate came to her rescue, for soon after Roberta entered Govardhan Rai's household her mother-in- aw suffered a stroke. The girls, all three of them, shriveled with fear and shock; they would vomit after administering their mother the bedpan, they sprained their wrists when they had to turn her in bed. The newly married Roberta came down from Pune, where her husband was posted, to take charge of her mother-in-law. Roberta's broad wrists handled everything with ease. Sensing her mother-in-law's embarrassment while on the bedpan, Roberta cracked jokes to assure her she didn't mind the sight and smell at all.

There is nothing as effective as a paralytic stroke to clear out all prejudice from one's system. Mrs. Rai became so dependent on Roberta that she wanted her, and only her, around her constantly. She told everyone as soon as she was recovered enough to talk, that if she was up and about within a month it was all because of Roberta, who had nursed her day and night.

Raghav Rai's worst fears came true when Tanya walked out on Rajiv. Too many cultural differences, diagnosed the Colonel. When matters started to go beyond repair, Rajiv began to share his grievances with his Dad. But even with him he did not share the final nail that sealed the coffin.

"I know you bathe everyday ....it's just that it seems that you do not," Tanya had said, referring to his swarthiness.

Rajiv did not retort. We quarrel only when there is still a possibility of a relationship. He was glad when she walked out.

The Colonel noticed that his son's voice didn't sound tired anymore when he spoke to him over the phone. He also marked that Rajiv wasn't uttering harami ka pilla every two minutes. He had shared his concern with Roberta:

"Rajiv says saala soowar ka baccha and harami in every second sentence....he must be really perturbed."

With Tanya gone, Rajiv intensified his search for Polly. One day when he was waiting at Boston airport Rajiv saw a familiar face rush past. She had not changed a bit – Jaishree Kapoor from Allahabad. She used to be a classmate of Polly's elder sister, Millie, and had gone to school in the same bus. Rajiv's own appearance had changed pretty much but she recognised him and met him with great warmth.

Somehow, Rajiv could not get himself to mention Polly. So he asked about Millie. Millie was fine, said Jaishree...she was in Bombay, she had been married to a pathologist when she was seventeen. Oh yes, she had her number in her phone. Jaishree hugged him and left.

"My search for Polly will be over at last," sighed Rajiv. Millie placed him instantly:

"Of course, I remember you!!!...What a pleasant surprise! I never thought I would ever hear from you!

A strange feeling of comfort spread through Rajiv.

Even in the past, everything associated with Polly had been dear to him: the bus that carried her to school, her milkman, her harridan of a mother, her Bigfoot of a father. All these years he had been drawn to women who had lips like Polly's, or eyes, or hair. He felt a sense of lightness and calm while talking to her sister, a sense of homecoming.

Soon he was telling her his story dipped in boastful lies, presuming that Millie would convey it all to Polly: how he had struggled since he was a teenager; the Americans had appreciated his expertise and had opened their country to him....now he was planning to buy a cottage, deep in the forest, and would travel to it in his own plane; his wealth, however, had been his bane, for it had attracted a completely worthless Latvian woman to him....he hadn't realized then that she was a nymphomaniac.... she was now with yet another man.

"I let the kids go because they resembled one of her lovers," lied Rajiv.

Rajiv hoped that these carefully drafted details about his life would be conveyed to Polly. He willed with all his heart that Polly would be unmarried, waiting patiently for him; and, if she was married, she would have lost her husband by now. Millie expressed regret over his matrimonial disaster.

"Was she American?" asked Millie "No. Swiss," said Rajiv not wanting to tell the truth.

Millie offered consolation:

"The loss is all hers. Nowhere would she have found a man as talented and handsome as you are."

"Oh come on!" said Rajiv, pleased.

"Seriously....in Allahabad they always spoke very highly of you."

"Well, I thought they thought me to be a Casanova."

Mrs. Sengupta's pejoratives still rung in his ears:

"You blighter, you useless bounder."

"No, no,....any girl would have given up the world to marry you. And you have proved how true you are....After all these years you have still not forgotten Allahabad."

From the way she uttered, "Allahabad" it seemed that she meant it to be a euphemism for his love affair that went awry, twenty years ago.

Then came her story:

"My mother-in law had seen me at a wedding. She decided that her son would marry me – and no other, for she thought I was the goddess Lakshmi in human form."

"Your daughter combines both beauty and virtue, Mr. Sengupta. She has such an auspicious air about her. Please, please, give me your daughter," recounted Millie, mimicking her mother-in-law. Millie continued:

"Many such potential mothers-in-law pestered my parents. They thought I would bring good fortune into their homes, my vibes were auspicious, they said. I wanted to study medicine but my parents succumbed to pressure – my mother-in-law insisted so much."

It was a long talk they had, across several continents and across oceans of time. Even then, Rajiv could not get himself to mention Polly. When he called Millie the following day he hoped she would talk about Polly. Millie seemed thrilled to hear from him. She greeted him with an effusive:

"Oh, I was waiting for your call. God knows why, I felt sure you would call."

After talking inanities, she suddenly asked him:

"Tell me: from the place you live, in America, how far are you from Philadelphia?"

"Not far... maybe a three hour drive. Why, do you have friends there?"

"No, no. No one. Just asking."

She did a great deal of talking but no mention of Polly. Disappointed and irritated, he decided he would call her next after a gap of two days. She began fretting when he called.

"I waited for your call all of two days. Was so worried that you might be sick or something." She then talked about all sorts of things – her new dhakkai sari -a gorgeous green, her adorable Labrador, her tailor who never kept his promise…. but no mention of Polly. He decided to seize the conversation. She was describing how difficult it was to bathe her dog ….she almost slipped and fell in the bathroom – he dodged her so much, when Rajiv cut her short abruptly, to ask about her family in Allahabad.

Millie spoke at length about her mother who was getting too old to live by herself. The father was in heaven; died of dehydration:

"He had heart trouble and we saw him through angioplasty and all that. Two months we ran around…….and then he died of dehydration, of all things! Had never liked to drink water. The only liquid that went into his system was in the form of tea or coffee. Come to think of it, had he not been so fond of tea…."

But still no mention of Polly. The following day he cut short her cooing:

"You had a sister…"

"Oh Polly ….she's fine, she's fine. This evening I have to go to my dentist…"

"Where is Polly these days?"

"Oh Polly….she is in Africa." Millie's voice sounded unsteady.

"Can you give me her phone number?"

"I'll have to see….you see she's very stuck up, I'll have to ask her before if I can give her number to anyone."

Rajiv was by now too annoyed to have anything to do with Millie. He decided he would not call her up anymore, not even at the risk of not getting Polly's number.

Not having heard from him four days, Millie called up Rajiv. She seemed frantic:

"Oh why have you not been calling. I am so sick with worry."

"I see no need for worry. I've been busy with my work," Rajiv replied coldly.

"Oh I have been missing you like anything....have you not missed me?'

"Why should I miss you?"

"How cruel of you to say that! Do you not love me?"

"Why should I love you? I hardly know you."

"You say that! After calling me every day, you say that! After convincing me that you loved me, you say that!" Millie was hysterical.

"I convinced you of no such thing, there is surely some mistake."

"Missstake!! You meet my friend at an airport and all you ask is about me; you take my number, call me up; for days you don't enquire about any other member of my family, you have ears only for me, and now you say there is some mistake! After all these years you have not forgotten me, and now you say there is some mistake!" Rajiv was speechless. She continued,

"Even twenty years ago I knew you had eyes only for me and that the letter you wrote was meant for me, even though that vain Polly imagined it was for her. Even in those days she went after every boy who liked me and I can guess that even now she is the one who is behind this sudden change in you."

"This is too much, lady. Where would I meet Polly – why, I don't even know where in Africa she lives."

"Africa!! You pretend she is in Africa when she is right there in Philadelphia, just an hour's drive from where you live.......I know it is she who is behind this sudden change in you.......You have ruined my life.......because of that letter you wrote me I was married off as soon as possible to the first man my father could catch hold of. Do you even realize that you have ruined me? Because of you I had to marry a man twice my age, a man who spends all his time looking at urine and faeces, only to come home late, then spend hours drinking with that awful friend of his – that Kapoor fellow. My friends tell me I look very good, but you should see how boring and dull my husband is. He may be wealthy, but wealth is not everything...."

Rajiv wasn't listening. Phew! It would be easy to track down Polly. He had Indian friends aplenty in Philadelphia. He would drive down the coming weekend. Philadelphia was, after all, only a three hour drive from New York.

6

Cordelia

Cordelia Gonsalves's father was posted to Allahabad for three years. So for three years we were classmates. Cordelia was very popular. She was a good-natured robust girl, a sportsperson and a tomboy. We were thirteen then; while the rest of us read Enid Blyton and Barbara Cartland, Cordelia had real romance in her life. She had met another Goan Christian like herself, Paul Fernandes, who was her mother's friend's son. Something sparked off between them; they were very happy together, cycling and playing tennis. Cordelia said that the sweetest thing in the world was to marry one's childhood sweetheart and she was sure that Paul and she would marry some day. Then three years passed, Cordelia's father was transferred away and we lost touch with her.

Several years later one of our classmates ran into Cordelia in a restaurant in Bombay. It belonged to her sister, Paula, who was elder to Cordelia. Paula ran a successful restaurant. To help her, the entire Gonsalves family had moved to Bombay. Cordelia was deeply attached to Paula's children aged five and three and even looked after them.

Cordelia was now engaged to Paul and their wedding was fixed two months hence. In the meantime, Paula had to make a business trip to Dubai. The entire family had gone to see her off at the airport. The children were excitedly pointing towards the plane which was carrying their Mamma. Just then, there was a loud burst and the plane crashed as soon as it took off. It was a terrible sight. And a most tragic one. The family was stunned for days to come. Paula's husband went silent and would not speak to anyone. It was then that Cordelia gathered courage and put all her heart to the upbringing of the children. The restaurant would have shut down had Cordelia not diverted her energies to its running. It was a most difficult period. Just then Paula's husband came to Cordelia with tears in his eyes and begged her to save his family by marrying him. There was no way Cordelia could refuse. The children were very attached to her. Paul Fernandes would find another girl to marry but the children would not find another mother like Cordelia.

ppp

7
Angrez Memsahib

(Part 1)

We begin in the India of the 1940s.

Bibi (Sardarni Rupinder Kaur), despite being a mother of two, still looked young and fresh. Her husband, Raja Singh, was a Civil Surgeon in the British Raj in the region of Sargodha, now in Pakistan. He was too busy to take care of his farms and properties in undivided India. Bibi would cover her head with her dupatta and get the farm produce loaded into her godown. Industrious woman she was, to travel five miles in a horse-drawn carriage to inspect the farms and orchards every fifth day of the week. The younger daughter, Tara, liked to skip school to accompany her mother to the farm where she would climb the haystacks; there was also a pokhara (pond) in which tadpoles swished their tails about, and dragonflies, always in doubt and indecisive, would suddenly turn towards the pond lily, or away from it.

The women on the farm would take Tara in their arms and would touch her silky hair; they would marvel at her frocks and her sandals. On one of these trips, Pir Baba – a Muslim mystic, came to the farm. He wore black robes and carried a bowl made of dried gourd. Pir Baba saw Tara and uttered in Hindi: "This child shall have two masters – one fair and one white; the fair one shall break her and the white one shall heal her."

Bibi turned red with annoyance, even as she dropped a coin into the gourd. She looked at her lovely daughter and tried to set her destiny straight with a stroke on her head. She set the prophecy aside at the utterance of a crazy man. Bibi dreamt of careers for her daughters in those times when marriage was the only possible career for women. She dreamt that at least one of her daughters would study medicine and make rounds in a hospital, wearing a white apron with a stethoscope round her neck. Equally strong was her desire to see her daughters happily married. Surely, since her husband held a respectable position, her daughters would find good husbands.

Indeed, Dr. Raja Singh held a position of great respect. The British officers – the City Magistrate and the Senior Superintendent of Police, would spend their evenings with him and even accepted invitations to dinner. Imtiaz Ali, a wealthy lawyer, was also part of the company. The relations between the Hindus, the Muslims and the Sikhs were good. On festivals, sweets would be exchanged. Raja Singh's mother, was, however, loathe to eat food sent by the Muslims, just in case it had been touched after touching forbidden items of meat. Whenever Imtiaz Ali would invite Raja Sigh for a meal, Raja Singh's mother would send along packed food for her son which he was supposed to eat at Imtiaz Ali's table. Of course, the tiffin never reached the table as Raja Singh would distribute the food amongst the servants.

Bibi had begun collecting items for her daughters' trousseau. Tara was only eight but the elder one, Hira, had crossed sixteen. Bibi embroidered sixty bedcovers, or khes. She had begun embroidering when the eldest one was born, and by the time Tara was eight sixty pieces of khes were ready. She had a special room constructed for them, which had no windows and but one door whose keys she threw away. The idea probably was to keep the khes untouched until the elder one would marry.

The city magistrate, Mr. Stew, made a sudden visit one evening. His body spoke of a certain urgency.

"Doctor," he said, sitting on the edge of the sofa, "We have news that riots have broken out between the Hindus and the Muslims in Bihar and Bengal and are fast spreading towards the North-West. The situation is nasty....I would advise you to move closer towards the East." Raja Singh said, "But all is calm here. I met Imtiaz Ali last evening. There was no mention of any rift."

"Yes, yes, it seems calm so far. But the Muslims are clamouring for this part of the country to be only for them. Sooner or later you will face violence."

"Where can I go? I have three houses here, a farm, several orchards, so many cows, buffaloes and servants. My bank accounts...."

"You are not safe here....you have young daughters too. I suggest you lock up and leave temporarily. If the situation improves you may return."

The doctor mentioned the matter to his family. His mother was outraged, "These Britishers want us out of this country itself! I have my gurudwara here....we are not going anywhere." Bibi said "The girls are receiving such good education here…we can't disturb them."

Two days later Bibi took Tara to the market to buy a frock-piece. Kallu the shopkeeper took out a pale blue with pink roses all over, saying "Bibi, this one will suit the little one very well." Suddenly there were sounds of panic. People were running down the street, smoke was billowing from behind the gurudwara. Bibi and Tara rushed home, leaving the frock piece on the counter. They soon learnt that Kallu had been beheaded.

There was blood everywhere, and smoke and fire; the cracking of wood as rafters fell; the shrieks of women and children. The temple bells and the muezzins fell silent. The gurudwaras were empty. Inside homes the kitchens were cold and the children sobbed with hunger.

In Raja Sigh's home bare essentials were packed into his car. The family was ready to flee. They landed in Rawalpindi from where they called up a cousin in Dehradun. The cousin asked them to reach Dehradun as soon as possible. Bibi kept the keys to the house in a vase, hoping they would return to their native home as soon as possible.

Had Raja Sigh's family entered Dehradun in happier times they would have found it beautiful. But they had come as refugees and it would take them some time to appreciate the greenery and the climate of this city at the foothill of the Himalayas.

Cousin Sattar Singh housed Raja Sigh's family with his own. Now there were twelve people in his home. Hospitality began to fall apart even though he was a generous man. There were twelve people huddled in four rooms.

The riots intensified on all the sides of the Punjab. The Muslims on the Indian side began to feel insecure, just as the Hindus and Sikhs had fled from the other side. There was Anwarul Hasan in Dehradun who left his beautifully furnished home with a garden huge enough to house sixteen varieties of mango alone, apart from lychees, peaches, pears and apricot in the backyard. The front garden was bright with poinsettia, phlox, and nasturtiums in spring. Two hundred pots of chrysanthemum stood in one corner of the lawn. Anwarul Hasan had a big room assigned for namaaz, nicely carpeted.

Among the Muslims was a Begum who lived in a similarly rich house. When the riots began she packed her belongings into a small bag. When her neighbour Seth Ram Das came to know of her plight he hid her in his home. He could have hidden her for a lifetime but the Begum was panic-stricken and wanted to leave this part of the country. And so she did.

It soon became clear that the religious divide was now very deep and there was no possibility of the Doctor's family of returning to their native place. The government allotted the homes of the Muslims who had left for Pakistan to the Hindu and Sikh refugees. That is how the Doctor's family moved into Anwarul Hasan's house along with two other refugee families.

The Doctor had little money and all refugees were dependent on the rations provided by the government. The refugees from the Punjab were accustomed to having rotis made of the famous wheat of their native land. But here the government could not afford providing wheat; it provided bajra instead. The refugees had black tea with little sugar and the children grew up on watered down milk.

Raja Saheb and Bibi refused to fret over not having sons. They tried to scrape money to educate their daughters. The elder daughter, Hira, had spent enough time in English medium schools in Punjab, but Tara was only eight when they came to Dehradun where she had to be enrolled in a Hindi medium school. Hira showed a great talent for art and a tutor was employed to hone her skills. Masterji, as the art tutor was known, was extremely talented, and he was planning to use his skills in a textile designing company. He suggested to Hira to enroll in one of the art schools in England.

Raja Singh was apprehensive of sending his daughter alone to a foreign country but Hira was too self-willed to be put down. She made arrangements for her passport and visa and with a heavy heart her family sent her off to Bombay from where she would board a ship to England. On board the ship were people from several nationalities. It was a long journey and people got to know each other. On board was a tall and handsome young man, a Muslim from Pakistan, by the name of Imran. He was a confident person who knew the ways of the world. Hira often turned to him for help whenever she had a problem. There struck a friendship between the two and both lamented the Partition. On her part was the loss of home and finances, on his part was the loss of friends.

Imran disembarked in Italy where he would spend a few days. He was employed in the Selfridges chain of departmental stores in Britain. Hira continued to sail on to Britain. It was autumn in England and her first taste of the country was a disappointing one. The weather was gloomy and dark and she felt daunted at the harbour. She did not know where to go. An Indian lady noticed her predicament and offered her a job as a domestic help. In her spare time Hira made frequent trips to Croydon, looking for an Arts school.

The job at the Indian lady's place was quite a comedown. The lady was very exacting and treated her as a menial.

The future looked bleak for Hira. One day when she was hunting for better prospects in and around Croydon she came across an English girl called Heather. Heather had been noticing Hira over a certain length of time and enquired as to what she required. Hira poured out her story. Heather offered her a place in her home. Hira was treated well by Heather but she saw no future for herself in England.

She finally phoned Imran and poured out her dejection. Hira decided to return to India. Imran arranged for her ticket and Hira was back again with her family.

It felt nice to be with her family, but fresh trouble began to brew when her parents began to pressurise her to get married. She turned down a couple of prospective bridegrooms –they were too orthodox. Having travelled abroad on her own, having seen the world, she would not fit into a typical Sikh family.

One day Hira went to an arts exhibition where she met a very pleasant young man – a Sikh called Kartar Singh. He struck up a good conversation with her. Kartar Singh began seeing her and soon proposed to her. Hira's parents were relieved that she had met a man of her choice and began to prepare for the engagement. They were rudely shocked when one day some men turned up saying that they were relatives of Kartar Singh's wife and not only was he married but had children as well. Raja Singh went along with the men to Kartar Singh's home to confirm, and found the allegation true. A harried looking woman struggled with two young children and there was Kartar Singh's photograph on the mantelpiece.

This jolt had a deep impact upon Hira. Meanwhile, the pressure of marriage was mounting and England seemed the only place to escape. This time Raja Sigh would not hear of it. His signatures were required for the visa. Hira's art teacher was a very good calligraphist. He agreed to forge Raja Singh's signature. This is how Hira escaped to England. Imran had come to the port to receive her. She told him all about her struggles. Hira was greatly relieved when Imran offered to marry her. Together they decided to set up a shop. They made a good team and were known as a happy couple considering that Sikhs and Muslims were daggers drawn in India.

Angrez Memsahib

(Part 2)

Tara

I first met Tara after my wedding, through my parents-in-law. She was already married to Ashley. They were both middle aged but youthful and both very charming. They threw a party for us newlyweds and laid out a great fare. Her home was warm and colourful, with the fire-place glowing. She looked perfectly in charge of her household. They looked happy together. They were both previously married and both had spouses and children from their earlier marriages.

There was much gossip against Tara, that she an Indian had abandoned her husband and children to marry a Britisher. There was a hint of greed in the gossip that she had married Ashley because Britishers were often richer than Indians. But Ashley looked too erudite to marry a woman without respecting her; she was too open and graceful to deserve such a charge. Years later I happened to be alone with her and the story came out.

Tara's story:

Hira had settled down in England and Tara was the only child left to bring up. Bibi complained to Raja Singh about Tara's poor education, for she was studying in a government Hindi-medium school. Being older, Hira had a better education than Tara, having been to a public school in Punjab. Tara's education was disrupted by the Partition.

Raja Singh sighed, "Let us wait for my practice to pick up." Raja Singh faced competition from other doctors in Dehradun. His cousin had died recently so the onus of the education of his four children also fell upon him. The family was struggling financially. Tara wore faded clothes, some hand-me downs too. But poverty cannot suppress beauty. Tara was now a pretty sixteen year old. She was indeed very charming.

A few houses away, on the same road lived the Kochars. They too were refugees but had left Punjab well in time to carry along their valuables and their money. Kocchar had been a timber merchant in Punjab and continued the same trade in Dehradun. They were wealthy and their children went to the best of schools. Their only son, Ranbir, was fair and sophisticated and drove a car.

Tara caught Ranbir's eye. She was very much in awe of him and that flattered him.

Ranbir completed his studies and got a good job in a carpet making company in Sirha, a village near Mirzapur. The factory was owned and run by two Britishers and everything was very English there. Ranbir began to feel lonely in his large house that was surrounded by tall trees. He spent his evenings drinking. He even slept around with the wives of some of the servants. On his next visit to

Dehradun, Ranbir met Tara again and felt a strong passion for her. He told his parents about his desire to marry her. The parents were not welcoming of this choice, considering Raja Singh's financial status. They also raised objections regarding Tara's ability to adjust to the westernised atmosphere in Sirha. "I will train her," said Ranbir. He had in mind her simplicity which would enable him to dominate her and also carry on with his extra-marital affairs.

Tara was on top of the world when Ranbir proposed to her. They got married through a simple wedding ceremony. The Company gave the newly-weds a warm welcome. Tara's happiness was short-lived; Ranbir began comparing Tara to the smart wives of the officers. Anger began to boil within him. He began nagging her for dressing slovenly and for speaking faulty English. He also told her to behave like a memsahib and not to enter the kitchen at all or do any household work. Tara was very confused. Nothing in her seemed right for Ranbir. She began to feel sick with anxiety and developed stress nodules.

When their first child, Sara, was born Ranbir would not allow the child to sleep in their bedroom. All night Tara would go to look the child up. It was too late to repent; Tara realised she had married a man with a heart of stone. When their first daughter, Sara, was eighteen months old Ranbir forced Tara to accompany him on a holiday leaving the child to menservants, despite Tara's protests. She was so sick with worry and disgust that she kept vomiting all through the holiday and had to be hospitalised. He complained that she had ruined his holiday.

Ranbir had married well for himself a girl who was too timid to oppose him and too weak to stand up on her own. Against her will he sent the children to hostel at an early age. The only good thing in this was that they would not see Tara being slapped and kicked by their father. He also laid it down that since he was going to spend so much money on their schooling they would not come home during the vacations to be influenced by their mother's slovenliness and Panjabi accented English. They would go to Ranbir's parents.

Difficulties were mounting for Tara. Ranbir had started bringing women home and sleeping with them in the bedroom. Tara would sleep in the guest room. Late one cold winter night Ranbir hit Tara hard and shut her out of the house. She stood amidst the trees, weeping. An employee passing by reported it to Ashley. Ashley had frequent reports from the servants how Tara Memsaheb was daily ill-treated by Ranbir. Ashley went out and took Tara to the Company Guest house nearby. "Don't be afraid. I will stand by you," said Ashley as he left.

Ashley Wood was a lonely man, though he tried not to show it. His wife, Vanessa, had left him, taking her children along to England. She preferred to live with John Brand who was infinitely Ashley's inferior in every way. She later told Tara that Ashley was the nicest man she knew but she liked to live with John.

Vanessa was very good-looking and Ashley loved her deeply. Perhaps that is the reason he let her choose her own happiness. He spent his lonely days reading. He had a brilliant library. The thought of Tara kept coming to his mind now and again. He was concerned about her but there was little he could do for her. Blow came upon blow, Ranbir left his job at Sirha and took up another job in, Ludhiana, which was far from Mirzapur. But his behaviour towards Tara remained the same. One day he turned her out of the house and asked her to leave him. He gave her a ticket to Dehradun and a ten rupee note. Bibi and Raja were heartbroken to see their beloved daughter in such a pathetic condition.

Tara began to look for jobs and found one as a secretary in a girls' school. She wrote a letter to Ashley informing him about all the latest developments in her life. They began corresponding with each other. Ashley's letters gave her a lot of strength. And soon, one day he came to meet her and the family members. His presence gave Tara much comfort.

After Vanessa left him, Ashley had planned to remain a bachelor. But Tara made him reconsider his decision. Through the servants Ashley had got frequent reports of the physical and emotional trauma Tara went through at Ranbir's hands. But Tara never showed it on her face. There was a perpetual smile on her lips. Ashley had seen the tenacity of Indian women towards their family. He admired them for their devotion towards their husbands. No Indian woman would do to her husband what Vanessa had done to him.

The thought of Tara frequented him. He began writing long letters to her. He told her how he had come to India for a casual visit but he liked the country so much he decided to stay on forever. He much preferred the bright sunshine of India to the long and gloomy winter of England. There was something spiritual about the Vindhyan Hills near Mirzapur. He loved it when in spring the hills would burst into the flame-of-the-forest. He wrote to Tara about the summer of England with poppies growing wild alongside roads and in farmlands. The mistletoe would glisten under the sunshine. He wished he could show her the blue of England's skies in and the green of her grass in summer.

Tara would write back about her childhood in the Punjab and the farms and orchards. She missed Sirha, especially the picnics to Wyndham and Amooi. What a lovely village Amooi was, at the foot of the hills.

Tara's parents were extremely upset about her life with Ranbir and suggested a divorce, to which she agreed. The divorce came through and Ashley proposed to her. Tara reminded him of the cultural differences between them. Ashley assured her that he liked her because she was an Indian. He also assured her of his care for her children. The court had allowed Tara to meet her children.

Ashley and Tara got married in the court. It was a day of resurrection for Tara. She had not imagined that a husband could give as much love and respect to his wife as Ashley did. He kept his promise regarding the children, who loved him in return. Later he played father of the bride at Sara's wedding and wore an Indian dress and a pink turban to give the bride away.

Bibi recalled the Muslim pir's prophecy, "...a white man shall heal her," as she saw Tara grow from strength to strength and become a confident person. There are certain things only love can do.

Tara's home in Sirha stands between Mirzapur and Barkacha. If you drive down too fast you are likely to miss it, so covered it is by trees. In winter look out for a creeper with rich red flowers in the corner. That's where her house is. I call it the House of Love for I have never seen such strong love as I saw between Ashley and Tara. It transformed her into a self-assured, confident woman. When I went for Ashley's funeral on a cold December morning his body was laid out in the veranda covered with flowers from the garden. Tara's eyes were swollen with weeping but she was, unlike most Indian women, well under control of herself, and meeting those who had come to mourn. She had put on Ashley's favourite "Lara's Theme."

That was so British on her part! On his part, Ashley had asked to be cremated in the country where he had spent fifty-six years. What better fusion of cultures could there have been in a country that had been partitioned for sheer lack of empathy and love.

❦❦❦

8
Gopal Chacha

We lived in a joint family, four uncles, one widowed aunt, seven cousins comprising four boys and three girls, in grandfather's spacious villa in Allahabad. Grandfather was a prosperous lawyer; all his offspring were married, but one. Gopal Chacha, the unmarried uncle had qualified for the Indian Administrative Services but preferred to join the University of Allahabad as a teacher of philosophy. Despite his father's wealth he financed his own education by giving private tuitions. He was that kind of an idealist.

There were several offers of marriage for Chacha but he was academically inclined and kept deferring the marriage. Then the family hunted out a beautiful girl, Sudha, from a wealthy family. They compelled Chacha to meet her and he agreed to marry her.

Chacha, being an introvert, had few friends; one Suresh Chandra befriended him. Suresh was Chacha's colleague in the Department of English in the University. He was the complete opposite of Chacha, an extrovert. Suresh was witty and smart and made us all laugh. He dressed like an Englishman and smoked expensive cigarettes.

Suresh kept visiting us every other day. He planned picnics and movies. We liked his visits and looked forward to his coming.

One day Sudha Chachi said she was going to the market and left a note on Chacha's study-table. She had eloped with Suresh. Chacha took the event philosophically but the family did not. They cursed the times and said great care should be taken while bringing up youngsters. Even though we cousins, whose ages ranged from sixteen to twelve, had nothing to do with the elopement the family burdened us with all the guilt, as if we were potential adulterers and home-breakers. Rules suddenly came up regarding the dresses of the girls; no more frocks, they would wear only salwar kameez. They were not to be seen on the terrace, nor heard talking over the phone. No more movies for us. A rather stern looking Brahmin called Dwivedi Mastersaheb was employed to read the Ramayana to us in the evening, which was kite-flying and cricket playing time.

Before the Elopement, ours was a relaxed and friendly family. But now even relatives were looked upon with suspicion. We youngsters began to feel claustrophobic and depressed especially when Mastersaheb lectured us on virtuosity. Sometimes we would go into fits of laughter out of sheer stress and boredom. When Mastersaheb would object we would point towards something as lame as a mosquito for an excuse for our laughter.

The sixteen year old, the eldest amongst us, Raju, said that if we became as pious as the family was trying to make us, we would become dreadfully boring and our spouses too would elope. Of course we were young and did not understand this loss but the word 'elopement' now sounded to us like a dark monster that had swallowed our family, sucked us into its darkness and had silenced our joyful laughter.

Suresh had to leave the University and Chacha got divorced from Sudha. The family got down to getting Chacha remarried, without consulting him. The women were of the opinion that since Sudha's beauty was the cause of all the trouble they would now look for a plain or ugly looking girl from a middle income group. They met several girls whom they had to reject on grounds of good looks. They could not advertise in the matrimonial columns for a plain looking girl. Ugly girls' parents would wonder why a pleasant looking man like Chacha would marry a plain looking girl. Raju came up with a bold statement that amongst married people elopements happened once in a million and that one chance should not be considered a rule. The family agreed with this point of sense. In the meantime, Chacha got fed up with the family and said he would choose his own bride. The aunts protested against this liberty saying he would choose the wrong person again. Chacha reminded them that Sudha was their choice, not his. In due course of time he made friends with a good looking girl and married her.

His marriage changed Chacha as a person. He began to laugh and talk more and dressed better. More importantly, he freed us all. Good days were back again as he requested Mastersaheb to leave and asked our parents to let us wear what we liked and do what we wished. "Don't punish them on account of the elopement." That was the last time we heard of that word at home. And Chacha lived happily with his new wife.

ppp

9

Listening to Rain

Born of loneliness I am the daughter of silence. Mine is a silence of the year around, marked only by little sounds which remind me that I AM.

On cold winter nights how often I have sat in my room searching for my soul's oasis in one of the four bare walls. The room is silent as though anticipating danger; its heart beats fearfully in the ticking of the clock. Somewhere outside, hid beneath the silent foliage of the night, a cricket teases me regularly,

"You are alone, you are alone, you are not only alone but also silent," which only adds despair to loneliness.

What if I am silent, Nature isn't. It is spring and there are new birds on the trees. They chirp excitedly, ever ready to LIVE. The receding sun, old and mild, stretches out its spiky hands to bless the tender young guava leaves, and the parrots, panic stricken, rush to the skies screeching. But why, what happened?

Summer so loveless, summer so stark....All the barrenness, hopelessness, frustration of mother Nature is compounded into a slow, still, sad wind that harps on the bare peepal twigs. I know this sound very well; it speaks of a restlessness, a suffering which one has to bear. The sound reminds us of the helplessness of mankind, in fact of all life, and it reminds us that we must bear with it, there is no escaping it.

What when the monsoon comes dripping down drop by drop from the lush, green trees. Their branches, dark and wet, look like a woman drenched in love.

The sky avenges all our helplessness and despair. It comes roaring down oppressively on the hedge-leaves which submit meekly to the intensity of its wrath. It is determined to subdue all recalcitrant elements. The power of the rain is supreme. Nature bows before it. Only an audacious crow sits obstinately on the telegraph wire. I see it for a moment, when lightning glows. All is dark and subdued. The sky keeps pouring down fiercely and as it thunders down I feel a new life in me. The hopeless despair which lay in my heart seems to be washing away. For no reason at all I feel light, I feel blithe, I feel happy. My mind undergoes a catharsis with the passionate outpouring of the emotions of the sky. Even the skies go wild sometimes. It is reassuring to know this.

Gradually the sky tempers down. Maybe it is tired, maybe ashamed of its uncontrolled passion. It continues to sob quietly.

Have you ever listened to the evening rain? I mean gentle rain. It comes down as a thin veil of silver. The air looks blue. The wind sends friendly little drops flying into your face. It is almost a token of love. The slight pattering of little drops on stone is a rhythm that lulls you to a waking sleep. Calm in body and in mind, you see eternity spread out in the quiet blue air. You feel the rain caressing the leaves. However, when big drops "blob" onto the banana leaves the story is different. The banana leaf asks, "You have come?

You have come?" The rain replies in a dry unemotional tone, "I am not going to stay." To The grass the rain makes soft promises of love, and it is rather noisy with a tin-roof like two school-boys boasting about themselves, none listening.

And as I sit on the steps, listening to the voice of the Rain that speaks regularly to the stones, the old questing keeps harping at me –what am I in this SILENCE? For when the sky has raged and poured, the gentle rain merges with the silence, becomes one with it. With every drop the rain nags me, "What are you in this silence."And I conclude that the rain is, like the cricket, after all a reminder of ever-present silence.

ррр

www.ingramcontent.com/pod-product-compliance
Lightning Source LLC
Chambersburg PA
CBHW062222150726
47991CB00006B/2393